To S[...]

With love,

[signature]

Ms. Amy Meislin Pollack has been writing as long as she can remember. From the time her fourth-grade teacher used to call her up to the front of the class to tell impromptu stories about a mischievous little girl named Jelly Bean, to her beginning to write down these stories. Throughout her many years of teaching many grades and many subjects (from elementary through college) through raising three children, she has always told stories, and continued writing them down.

She currently lives with her husband in central New Jersey, and enjoys reading, writing, walking, and spending time with her husband, her children and six grandchildren.

This book is lovingly dedicated to Marty, David, Jake, Becky, Nancy, Carol, Hannah, Brody, Isla, Jamie, Zoe and Remi.

Amy Meislin Pollack

THE ADVENTURES OF
JELLY BEAN

AUSTIN MACAULEY PUBLISHERS™

LONDON * CAMBRIDGE * NEW YORK * SHARJAH

Ordering Information
Quantity sales: Special discounts are available on quantity purchases by corporations, associations, and others. For details, contact the publisher at the address below.

Publisher's Cataloging-in-Publication data
Pollack, Amy Meislin
The Adventures of Jelly Bean

ISBN 9781649793720 (Paperback)
ISBN 9781649793713 (Hardback)
ISBN 9781649793737 (ePub e-book)

Library of Congress Control Number: 2022900774

www.austinmacauley.com/us

First Published 2022
Austin Macauley Publishers LLC
40 Wall Street, 33rd Floor, Suite 3302
New York, NY 10005
USA

mail-usa@austinmacauley.com
+1 (646) 5125767

I'd like to thank my children – David, Jake and Becky - for their unflagging support all these many years. I love you all more than you can know. Becky especially (since my story is about a young girl, and she was – and is – my one girl) has given me helpful ideas and suggestions when I was stuck, and which made me say "ah yes," of course. A big thank you is in order to all my students over the years for helping me understand many kinds of children and young adults. They helped me to see why they say and do what they say and do, and to begin to understand why they behave the way they do.

Thank you, in memoriam, to my parents, who were gone too soon, but remembered with love everyday. In many ways this book is an ode to them. I once took them for granted, but I have come to realize and herein I've tried to show how they made my childhood nothing short of idyllic. They were unusual. And then my grandparents, long gone but remembered in rich detail, are here, rolled into one. All three of them were integral parts of my early life. I only wish I could have known my father's father, who died long before I was born, and who sounded utterly fascinating.

A big thank you to my grandchildren – Hannah, Brody, Isla, Jamie, Zoe and Remi – who I hope will one day realize all they've contributed to my world, and how they have enabled me to embrace a whole new dimension. Could the grandmother in the story be me? I like to think so (in part, anyway). Hannah, I am especially grateful to, for listening patiently to all my drafts, and for always offering extremely helpful advice.

Thank you to my cousin Ariel Meislin, for all her amazing help and patience in showing me how and where to submit my young adult story. I owe her a huge debt of gratitude for helping me get it noticed.

Thank you to our dogs, who have enriched our lives with their loyalty, as well as their abilities to soothe and provide steady companionship. They are man's (and Jelly Bean's) best friend.

Thank you to Carol, my husband's cousin and "birthday buddy," who was the first model for this Jelly Bean, because she is the youngest of four and has three older brothers. When I first knew her, I thought what an interesting and sometimes challenging situation, but one so different from my own – and so worth exploring. She is so full of fun with her ready laugh, willingness to share, and ability to be her own person.

Thank you to my sister Nancy Siegel, who is never too busy to listen and offer wise counsel. She's simply the best sounding board anyone could wish for.

Thank you to my mother-in-law Pauline Pollack, now gone but not at all forgotten, who always encouraged me to keep writing my "children's stories," and whose persistent reminders made me want to write this to conclusion.

Thank you to Miss Layla Gramiccioni – one of my most avid young "beta" –readers, who offered some helpful suggestions and comments.

Thank you to my editors at Austin Macauley Publishers Ltd. In helping to bring my story to fruition.

And, finally, huge thanks go to my husband, for his constant support and especially for his help with the technological aspects of my writing process, which often manage to elude me. Marty I love you.

Chapter 1
Jelly Bean Has a Rough Day

As if being the youngest in the family weren't difficult enough, Jelly Bean had the added challenge of having to grow up with three older brothers. One might have been bad enough, and two would probably have been a little more irritating – but three was often unbearable. Like when everyone acted as if what she had to say was not important. Or just plain stupid. Sometimes everyone laughed – when what she said wasn't meant to be funny. Whenever one of the boys had something to say, Mom and Dad really listened. When Jelly Bean said something, it felt like no one paid much attention. Most days it seemed like the only one in her household who had any sympathy for her was Roger-Over, who was simply the best dog in the whole wide world. In the human category Sam, her middle brother, sometimes had time for her. He could be sympathetic too. When he was around.

But today was turning out to be an all-around next-to-impossible day for Jelly Bean. In the first place, she started off the day by getting to school late, because of something that happened which was too dumb and embarrassing to explain to Ms. Peiser, her teacher. Right when her carpool was just about at the house, and Jelly Bean had already put on her jacket and backpack, she had to use the bathroom.

"Hurry, honey," Mom had called out. "I'll tell Gale to wait." Mom didn't exactly sound thrilled.

Jelly Bean had been in such a hurry, though, she forgot to check whether the toilet lid had been left up – which was how the boys were always leaving it. Mom was constantly telling Michael, Sam, and Joel not to, but they still left it up all the time. And as Mom was always saying, "Boys will be boys." So just when Jelly Bean needed to run out the door, instead she found herself in the toilet. In freezing-cold water.

"Ma!" she wailed. "Maaaaa, tell Gale to wait for me!" Jelly Bean ran to her room to change her clothes. Since her tights were wet, she realized she had to change her skirt and her top, because the top she had on didn't match the skirt she had changed into. Then her sweater didn't match. And now her hair was all messed up from putting the new sweater over her head. Yelling and almost tripping over Roger-Over, Jelly Bean pulled opened her dresser drawers and closet bins, throwing tops, tights, skirts and pants all over the place. Nothing she put on looked right, even the new clothes Mom had just bought her. Some of the popular girls had started to make fun of what she was wearing the first few weeks of school. Some of them had told her her clothes were so last-year. She should have waited to buy clothes till she saw what everyone else was wearing. Something about each and every piece of clothing just wasn't right.

She finally put an outfit together, but when she looked in the mirror, she burst into tears. The top that said "Love" in big letters looked dumb, the new skirt she had on was way too long, and now her eyes were all red. On top of everything, she was going to be late. Very late. She heard Mom yell out to Gale to go ahead, that she would have to take Jelly Bean a little late. Today was turning out to be hopeless.

Jelly Bean heard the fast pat-pat of Mom's flip-flops heading her way.

"Jillian, what happened to you?" Mom would ask a dumb question at a time like this. Mom and Dad were the only ones – besides Grandma and Grandpa – who still called her by her real name. "Oh dear," said Mom, looking half-amused, half-disgusted. "This room looks like a tornado just hit."

Mom was not in an understanding mood at all. "It's getting late, Jilly," she said. "We really need to leave."

Jelly Bean quick pulled her boots back on. "I'm going as fast as I can," she told Mom. "And I know it's not a good time to tell you this," she said, grabbing her backpack and following Mom glumly down the stairs, "but none of the clothes we bought before school started are any good."

"Good heavens, Jillian," Mom practically yelled, stopping by the kitchen to text someone, "please don't say such silly things to me."

Jelly Bean followed Mom down the stairs from the kitchen to the garage, threw her backpack in the back seat and went around to climb into the front. She gave up on the clothes problem, for now. "Ms. Peiser's choosing everyone for the good parts in the class play today, first thing," she told Mom. "She said if someone wasn't in class on time today, they had no chance of getting a good part, and not to even bother asking."

Mom sighed, shook her head, and drove. "I can try calling," Mom offered.

When they pulled up to school, Jelly Bean sunk down in her seat and folded her arms. "I don't think I can even go to school today," she said. "I'm nauseous."

"Jillian, you're fine," said Mom. "It'll all work out, it always does. I promise."

"You always say stuff like that," Jelly Bean told her. Mom shook her head.

"How late am I?" Jelly Bean asked, hauling her backpack from the back. She groaned.

"At this rate, Jilly, you'll never get there," said Mom. "And I'm going to miss my appointment." Mom was getting to be as cold as ice. She looked down at her nails.

"Okay, I get it. My problems aren't all that important to you. Give your daughter a break, huh?"

Mom scribbled a note and handed it to Jelly Bean. It told the ladies in the office that she was late because of an emergency. "Kiss," said Mom.

Jelly Bean gave Mom a kiss and got out of the car slowly. "I can't go in there!" she turned around and told Mom, just as she was about to drive off.

Mom shook her head. "Drama queen," she said to her.

"Am not," said Jelly Bean. Jelly Bean made an unhappy face before she turned around and headed into the school building. She handed her note to the office ladies to sign.

Then she ran down the hall as fast as she could, with her ridiculously heavy backpack slamming against her back.

"...and the rest of the class will be in the chorus," Ms. Peiser was saying, as Jelly Bean slinked into the back of the classroom. Unfortunately, she had to walk to the front of the room, with everyone's eyes on her, to hand in her note. Ms. Peiser tossed the note on her desk, not even bothering to look at it. She continued, motioning to Jelly Bean to sit down: "...so when the people with speaking parts are rehearsing on stage, those of you in the chorus will go to Mr. Klein's room to learn your songs. All right now –" Ms. Peiser had to stop speaking and clap her hands together until the class quieted down. Jelly Bean got up all her courage, and quickly walked back up the row of desks to the front of the classroom.

"Ms. Peiser," she began, but some of the pushy boys and girls immediately crowded her out.

"Everyone sit down immediately," said Ms. Peiser, "and those who have questions can come see me at recess. That's all the time we have to discuss the play right now. Everyone needs to get out their math homework, quickly. And open your books to page 93."

Jelly Bean's mind was too busy to jump right into math.

She desperately needed to find out from Taylor Alpert, who sat next to her, if all the speaking parts had been given out already – or at least if she had any chance of getting one. Otherwise, she'd have to wait until recess, which was light years away, to try to get to Ms. Peiser to ask her.

"Will you please wait a second, Jelly Bean?" Taylor was in the middle of folding up a huge piece of construction paper in a big hurry that she threw over to Shelby Trankman, the girl who sat on her other side. Taylor just wasn't the friend she used to be. She had changed so much, and had gotten so mean since the beginning of school, that now she seemed like a completely different person.

"Miss Kramer," Ms. Peiser said sternly, "first you come in late. Then right away you begin to disrupt the class." She gave Jelly Bean a disgusted look. If only she could explain to Ms. Peiser exactly what had happened so far that day.

Jelly Bean felt her face growing hotter and redder. On top of everything else, Taylor was whispering something to Shelby and they were both laughing! How awful, to be singled out and yelled at in front of the class, while the girl who was supposedly your best friend was whispering about you and laughing. "Miss Alpert," said Ms. Peiser, sounding even angrier, "if you think this is so funny, you can join Miss Kramer on the trip she is about to take to Mr. Johnston's office. Right now, girls!" Ms. Peiser was in the worst mood Jelly Bean had ever seen her in. She made a big show of picking up the phone receiver on the wall by her desk, and telling the office people that two girls with bad behavior were on their way down.

Out in the hall, Jelly Bean had trouble keeping up with Taylor. "Hey Tay, wait up," she called.

"Walk faster slow-poke," Taylor called over her shoulder, pushing in the heavy swinging door, and letting it swing right back onto Jelly Bean. Jelly Bean walked as quickly as she could down the stairs, but Taylor had already skipped to the bottom of the second staircase.

"Where are you going, Jelly Bean?" Joel, her brother who was in seventh-grade called out, who just then happened to be coming up the stairs – out of nowhere – with two of his friends. They were passing Jelly Bean and Taylor going in the opposite direction, carrying a large screen and some other audio-visual equipment. The middle school where Joel went was connected to Jelly Bean's elementary school, for some ridiculous reason. She barely ever ran into him or his creepy friends, but of course today had to be the one time she did.

"Just going to the office to get something for our teacher," Jelly Bean called out. Phew, that was fast thinking.

"No we're not, Jelly Bean," Taylor called from the bottom of the stairs. "Our teacher's sending us to Mr. Johnston's office because we were bad!"

"Naughty fourth-graders," Joel's friends teased, as they rounded the bend at the top of the stairs.

"Come on you guys, let's go," said Joel. "Ooooh, Jelly Bean," he turned around to say to her, "wait till I tell Mom and Dad tonight." The three of them went speeding away, almost crashing into one another.

"Thanks you idiot," Jelly Bean called after him, but not loud enough for him to hear. Could this day get any worse?

"Ha ha," laughed Taylor, who stood facing Jelly Bean, her back against the door. "I'm glad I don't have any sisters or brothers to tell my parents on me!"

"Please tell me if I have a chance for a speaking part, Taylor!" Jelly Bean heard herself asking, instead of thinking up something clever to say back to her. But nothing like that ever popped into her head.

"How could you expect to get a part, dumbbell? You didn't get to school on time today, remember? What was going on anyway, while we were waiting for you in the car?" Taylor was giving her a funny look. A nasty look. Tears kept fighting their way into Jelly Bean's eyes, but she wiped them away before they could dribble down her cheeks. She gritted her teeth.

"You're dense," said Taylor.

"Nothing happened, okay?" Jelly Bean finally answered.

"Yeah right," said Taylor. "We heard you yelling for your mother." This was the new Taylor, the mean Taylor, enjoying watching Jelly Bean get upset. Some best friend.

Jelly Bean didn't answer. She did try hard, though, to swallow the lump that kept forming in her throat as they approached the principal's office. It stuck there though, and wouldn't budge. Taylor calmly opened the door. If she tried to speak, Jelly Bean knew she would start crying.

"Are you the fourth-graders sent down to see Mr. Johnston?" asked Mrs. Milano in her too-loud voice. It was so embarrassing when everyone in the office turned around to stare, from the secretaries looking over their little eyeglasses to the two janitors standing in the corner holding packages, to a few other kids with their coats and backpacks on holding notes explaining why they needed to be excused early that day.

Jelly Bean couldn't answer. She just kept looking down at the tiles on the floor. But Taylor didn't seem upset at all. She looked like she was enjoying the attention. Jelly Bean wished she could disappear through one of the cracks between the tiles.

"Yup, that's us," Taylor answered, leaning her elbows on the counter, which she was just able to reach when she stood on tiptoe. "Is he out today or something? M.I.A.?" Taylor wasn't afraid of anyone or anything. And even though Taylor had been so mean to her lately, still Jelly Bean couldn't help admiring her now. She was one of the only people in the fourth grade who wasn't afraid of Mr. Johnston. And he was scary. "We have to get back to class. Tell him we waited as long as we could." Then, surprise of surprises, Taylor jumped up and pushed herself forward onto the counter.

"Get down from there, young lady," Mrs. Milano said sternly, moving her large body from her desk to the counter.

She glared at Taylor. "Now sit down quietly and wait until Mr. Johnston can see you," she scolded them both.

Mrs. Milano looked at the other two office ladies, and shook her head. They both looked back at her, rolling their eyes. Then they looked at Taylor with the nastiest expressions ever. They mostly ignored Jelly Bean, but her heart was beating so loud she was sure everybody could hear it.

"Taylor, just listen," Jelly Bean tried again. But instead of sitting down next to her, like she would have in the old days, Taylor stood facing Jelly Bean, and tried to do the splits. "My mother called the school," Jelly Bean tried to explain. "She told them I was going to be late. She told them to tell Ms. Peiser that I really wanted to have a chance to get a good part, I just needed to be a little bit late because—"

"Ow!" screamed Taylor, who had just fallen backwards on the office floor, and was laying there rubbing her elbow. "That really hurt. I wonder how

14

Shelby does it so perfectly." There it was again – Taylor trying to copy Shelby: the way she talked, the way she dressed, the way she ignored some people, and was nice to certain others. But the most annoying thing of all about Taylor was her copying the way Shelby was always practicing doing the splits, every chance she got. That was because she had an older sister who was a cheerleader at the high school. Funny thing was, Jelly Bean noticed, the more Taylor tried to get Shelby's attention, the more Shelby ignored her. Why were people acting so strange this year? Third grade had been so different, Jelly Bean thought to herself. It used to be easier to predict the way people were going to act. Now it was so hard to figure out what to do. Maybe she'd have to change and act different; but if she did have to, then how, she wondered…

"If your mother really called the school, why don't you ask Mrs. Milano over there if she gave Ms. Peiser the message?" said Taylor. "Maybe she forgot. She's only human, you know," Taylor was saying in a really loud voice. Mrs. Milano glared at them, and looked as disgusted and mean as Jelly Bean had ever seen an adult look. Her look was even worse than Ms. Peiser's when she was on the warpath, when people in the class were really behaving terribly. Mrs. Milano looked like she was about to say something else to the two of them, but luckily, she had to go answer the office phone.

"What can I do for you girls?" Mr. Johnston, who had just come into the office, stared at the two of them with a no-nonsense look and his arms folded tightly. In his office, while he lectured them about things that might happen if they didn't behave, Jelly Bean sat completely still on the bench across from him, not even daring to look around. Taylor, on the other hand, was swinging her legs and yawning. She even burped twice.

"Jelly Bean, what are you so afraid of?" she said to her once they were out in the hall. Mr. Johnston had told them this was their last warning before he was going to call their parents. "It's not like we were found with drugs or anything."

"I know," Jelly Bean said, "but still—"

"What is your problem? Why are you such a scaredy-cat? What did you think that old guy was going to do, send us to student jail or something?"

Jelly Bean laughed, but her heart was still pounding.

Then on the way back to class, she had trouble walking as slowly as Taylor was. Now she was stopping on each step, and trying to do the splits every few seconds.

"Why are you waiting for me?" Taylor asked. "I thought you wanted to get back so you could bug Ms. Peiser about not getting a part."

"I know I'm not going to get a speaking part," said Jelly Bean. No answer. "And how come you're walking so slow, Tay?"

"Because I'm not in the mood for math or science," Taylor answered slowly, taking teeny-tiny steps, "and if I time things right, I'll get back just in time for recess." She lounged against the wall, and slid down to the ground. Then she jumped back up.

For the rest of the day, Taylor either ignored Jelly Bean or started whispering and laughing with someone else when Jelly Bean was nearby. And as far as Shelby went, there was something about her this year that made all the girls want to be around her and act like her. They all wanted her to like them. Today at lunch, when Jelly Bean went to her usual seat, which happened to be at Shelby's table, it was taken by someone else. And that someone else was Britney Keller, the meanest girl in the entire grade.

"Britney—" Jelly Bean started to say, to try to get Britney to give her her seat back. But before she could say anything else, Britney turned around and gave Shelby a look. That look told Jelly Bean she was going to have to sit someplace else.

"Jelly Bean," said Shelby finally, looking up at her, with a look as nasty as any look Jelly Bean had ever seen, "do you think you could find another seat?"

Banished from her seat at the lunch-table. A large knot formed in Jelly Bean's stomach, as she wandered around with her tray, looking for a place at another table.

"Sure," answered Lara Newman, a chubby redhead, when Jelly Bean asked whether she could sit at her table. Probably no one had ever asked her that question before. And what a table too – four girls who not only still played with dolls but actually brought their dolls to school, and, of all things, pretended to be feeding them during lunch. Greg Westons sat with them too. Good old Greg with his old man's tortoise-shell glasses, who never cared where he sat, as long as he could read his book and pick his nose in peace.

"Where's your doll, Jelly Bean?" Taylor said, as she just happened to be passing by with her tray, on the way to her seat at Shelby's table. Jelly Bean looked down at the gooey mess of noodles and cheese on her plate, which she didn't even bother to pick at. The tears welling up in her eyes were making everything around her blurry, no matter how hard she pressed her hands over her eyes to try and stop them.

At least she'd try to solve one problem, Jelly Bean thought to herself, as her class raced out of the cafeteria after lunch. She wouldn't leave school – even if it meant missing her ride and having to walk all the way home – until she had spoken to Ms. Peiser about the play. There didn't seem to be much you could do about some things, but others at least you could try to fix.

"Here, Jelly Bean," said Heather Farrell, as they all stood outside the classroom waiting for Ms. Peiser to come open the door. Heather was a kind, short-haired girl whose house Jelly Bean had been to once, a long time ago, back in kindergarten.

"I saved you my piece of cake," Heather was saying, "because I noticed you weren't eating anything for lunch. Aren't you hungry today?" They stood together outside the classroom for a few moments while everyone else clambered in.

"Thanks, Heather.   Thanks a lot," said Jelly Bean. This was the nicest thing that had happened to her in forever.   "I wasn't too hungry during lunch," she told her, wondering whether Heather guessed the real reason why she hadn't eaten. "I sure am now though!" she told her.

The two girls sat in the small alcove outside their classroom, while Jelly Bean gobbled down the piece of cake. It was angel food, which she didn't really like, but this piece tasted pretty good.

"I wish I had some milk!" Jelly Bean said when she finished, and she and Heather both laughed. "Do you want to come over my house this weekend Heather?" Jelly Bean asked. "My brother got some new video games," she added. "He said I could use them. Well, actually my mom told him he had to share them with me."

"I'd love to!" Heather said. She looked so happy. Who cared that Taylor and the other girls were being mean to her, Jelly Bean told herself – although it wasn't exactly as simple as that. She really did care. They were the ones Jelly Bean wanted to have as friends. "I'll call you tonight, after I ask my mom," Heather was saying. They hurried into the classroom.

"Ms. Peiser," Jelly Bean called out, scurrying over to where Ms. Peiser had stopped on her way into the classroom. She was standing by the desks in the back talking to Mr. Singer, the fifth-grade teacher, in a low voice. "I need to ask you—" Jelly Bean continued.

"What do you say when you interrupt someone else's conversation?" asked Ms. Peiser sternly. Her arms were folded, and the way her elbows stuck out of her white rolled-up sleeves made them look like two sharp knives. But it was now or never, Jelly Bean thought to herself, and she forced herself to go on. And besides, teachers interrupted kids' conversations all the time.

"I mean, excuse me, Ms. Peiser, I have to ask you something really quickly about the play. See, this morning the reason I was late was because I have three older brothers, and one of them always leaves the toilet seat up, and I never know which one, but anyway I was all ready to leave for school, but I had to go to the bathroom, and I forgot to check, and, and, all of a sudden—" Jelly Bean had to slow down for a minute to catch her breath, "there I was in the toilet, so I had to go change all my clothes, since everything was soaking wet, and I wanted a speaking part so badly, so I asked my mom to call the school, but I don't think you got the message from her, because—" Jelly Bean looked from Ms. Peiser to Mr. Singer and back again, and saw they were laughing. How awful! They were both standing there looking down, laughing at her. Suddenly her cheeks were burning hot, and she knew they were bright red.

"Oh, Jillian!" Ms. Peiser shook her head and giggled, giving Mr. Singer a funny look. "I'll talk to you later, Al," Ms. Peiser said to him, as she kneeled down to talk to Jelly Bean. "I'll see what I can do, Jillian, but I can't make any promises. If your mother did call the school, as you said she did, I didn't get the message. And, the problem is, just about everyone would like a good part in the play, but plays generally don't have enough speaking parts for all the people who want them. And now all the parts have been given out. But I understand your – problem—" Ms. Peiser opened her eyes in a funny way. "So remind me first thing tomorrow morning, okay? I'll see if there's anything I can do." She took a tissue out of her skirt pocket, and dabbed at Jelly Bean's eyes. "So for now, just try to relax."

That was the nicest thing about Ms. Peiser: when you managed to catch her in the right mood, she did know how to make you feel better.

"Hi Jelly Bean!" said Heather, running up to her after the last bell had rung, and everyone was waiting outside near the driveway for their rides. Heather was out of breath from running. "I was calling you, but I guess you didn't hear me."

"Oh hi, Heather," said Jelly Bean. She didn't want to turn around, because Taylor was standing right behind her with Shelby and her group of friends.

"There's my mom. I'll go ask her about this weekend. Mom…" Heather opened the door of the bright red car that had just stopped in the driveway. "Can I go to Jelly Bean's house this weekend?"

"Oh hi, Jillian," Heather's mother called to her. Her short gray hair was poking up all over the place, which made her look like some creature from another planet. "That should be okay. Let Heather call you tonight honey," she said to Jelly Bean, "and you girls can make your plans."

After Heather's mom drove off, Jelly Bean was left alone, surrounded by the talking and laughing groups of boys and girls. Suddenly one boy bumped into her, hard. It was Jaden, who had been pushed by some of the other boys.

"Ow!" said Jelly Bean.

"What do you say when you bump into someone?" asked Mr. Jackson, the boys' gym teacher, quickly walking over to Jaden, who was laughing with his group of friends. Now he looked at the ground and shuffled his feet around.

"Sorry," he mumbled, not sounding like he meant it. Then he looked over at his friends to make sure they were all still laughing. They were. Jelly Bean wished she could disappear. When Taylor's mom pulled up, Jelly Bean and Taylor climbed into the back. Then Olivia, who barely ever said anything, got into the front.

"How did the day go?" asked Mrs. Alpert. She asked the same question every day.

"That dumb question again?" Taylor answered, rude as usual. Jelly Bean always wondered how come Taylor's mother never did anything about the way she acted towards her, which was always terrible. Once Jelly Bean's mom had told her the reason she didn't say anything was because she and her husband had wanted to have a child for a long time, and they finally had Taylor when they were pretty old. It didn't seem like a good reason. But sometimes adults were hard to figure.

"Are you taking me shopping now?" Taylor asked, which was also the same thing she always asked.

"Sure honey, where would you like to go?" Taylor's mom answered. She did look a lot older than Mom did. Mom had also told her that Mrs. Alpert couldn't have any more kids, which was another reason why she let Taylor do and say whatever she felt like. Jelly Bean wondered whether Taylor's mom realized she was getting brattier and brattier. Or whether she just didn't care.

"Bloomies. As fast as you can get there," Taylor was telling her mom. "I'm in a rush today. I need clothes. Badly." She leaned forward and burped loudly – right in Olivia's ear.

"Taylor," said Olivia, but so softly you could barely hear her.

"What?" asked Taylor, putting both her feet up on Olivia's side of the car. Then she pushed herself down far enough in her seat to be able to bend her knees over Olivia's seat, and klunk her over the head with her boot. All Olivia did was unfasten her seatbelt and move far enough forward to be out of the way of Taylor's moving boot.

"Taylor, sweetheart," was all her mother said, "please stop doing that."

"Doing what?" asked Taylor.

Jelly Bean used to think it'd be great to have a mother like Taylor's mom. But now she decided she liked her own mother better, even when Mom wasn't always the most patient person around. Still Jelly Bean knew deep down she was better off with the mom she had. Even though she didn't always feel like admitting it.

When Taylor's mom dropped Jelly Bean off at her house, Taylor didn't even bother saying good-bye. She started humming something instead. But when Jelly Bean saw Uncle Jack's car parked in the driveway, she didn't care about Taylor, or school, or just about anything else. She raced inside, threw down her backpack, and ran from one room to the other.

"Uncle Jack," she called. "Where are you?"

Chapter 2
Uncle Jack

"He's out back playing basketball with Michael and Sam," said Agnes, who came to clean the house a few days a week, and was on her way out the door as Jelly Bean was coming in. She was from a country where they only spoke Spanish, so she had a strong accent and sometimes Jelly Bean had trouble understanding her. Agnes couldn't speak English very well, but Mom had told Jelly Bean that English was a tough language to learn, and that Agnes was working on it at her night school. Agnes was so nice though, and always tried to talk to Jelly Bean about people on different crazy TV shows she watched when she got home. She also liked asking Jelly Bean what certain words meant.

"Bye Agnes!" she called after her, then shot through the house like a bullet, and out the door that led to the backyard from the kitchen. It shut behind her with a loud bang.

"Hi Uncle Jack!" she screamed toward the driveway, which was on the side of the house, where the basketball net was. It was really unfair that Michael and Sam, who were both in high school, got out of school so much earlier than she did. Sometimes they had sports or did other things that older kids did after school, but Jelly Bean's school didn't end until 3:15, which always made the school day feel like it lasted forever. Dad said that one day time was going to start going by really fast, but so far the only days when that ever happened were Saturdays and Sundays. Dad also said a lot of things in life were unfair, but that didn't help too much either.

"Jillian!" Uncle Jack called, smiling his big wide smile, as he ran towards Jelly Bean, grabbed her and lifted her high into the air. The yard spun around and around. Uncle Jack was studying to be an orthodontist, and as soon as he finished with his school, he was going to open an office and start putting braces

21

on kids' teeth. Mom said he'd probably get along with his patients just fine, since he himself acted like an overgrown kid most of the time.

"Help! Put me down!" Jelly Bean yelled, pounding on Uncle Jack's back and kicking her legs. It was scary but kind of fun at the same time, twirling around and around in the air like that. Uncle Jack was so tall, and as she spun around, the trees with their floppy branches circled all around her. Uncle Jack made Jelly Bean feel special. Like now for instance, when he put her down and told the boys to continue their game without him. Out of breath, he walked with Jelly Bean back into the house.

"Let me walk on your feet!" said Jelly Bean. Uncle Jack lifted her up in front of him, and set her down so that she was standing on his feet, while she faced him. Then he walked backwards, through the kitchen to the den, through the living room, into the dining room and back into the kitchen. Jelly Bean was laughing and shrieking, and that made Roger-Over dart in from the den, where he had been sprawled out on the rug, to check out the commotion and start barking like a lunatic. He pushed himself up to Jelly Bean and she hugged him and tousled his fur. He was a lovable mutt.

"So what's new in your young life?" asked Uncle Jack, catching his breath, as Jelly Bean stepped backward off his feet and plunked into a kitchen chair. She threw off her coat because now she was all sweaty, while Uncle Jack grabbed a box of doughnuts that was sitting on the counter waiting to be eaten. He took a container of milk from the refrigerator, and grabbed two glasses from the cabinet.

"Everything went wrong today," Jelly Bean told him, since he was one of the few people who was usually interested in what she had to say. After they asked her a question, most adults just pretended to care about the answer. Some didn't even do that and just got busy going back to what they had been doing before they asked.

"No kidding," said Uncle Jack. He turned one of the kitchen chairs around and threw his long legs around both sides of it. He finished the second half of his doughnut in one bite, and chose another one from the box.

As Jelly Bean carefully explained everything that had gone wrong that day, Uncle Jack nodded seriously, polishing off three more doughnuts while he listened.

"You know something?" Uncle Jack poured a tall glass of milk, and drank it down. Jelly Bean loved it when Uncle Jack kept her company after school.

Mom had told her that Grandma and Grandpa wished he would find a really special girl and settle down. "I had a terrible day too," he said, unexpectedly.

"You did?" Jelly Bean asked him.

"Yeah. Two of the patients I was working on complained about their braces today. And it was right when my department head came in to observe me."

"How come they complained about their braces?" Jelly Bean asked.

"Probably because they hurt. Braces hurt for a while when you first get them on. Remember that happening with your brothers? And some patients just complain a lot. Other patients are happy with them and don't complain much, but they weren't the ones who happened to be there today," he told her. Uncle Jack looked down and rocked back and forth a little in his chair. If Mom were there, she'd remind Uncle Jack these chairs weren't meant for rocking.

"What did you say to them?" Jelly Bean asked, picturing in her mind Uncle Jack's dental chair. She had even sat in it once when she visited his school with Mom and Dad. Uncle Jack had shown them all around, with a big smile on his face the whole time.

"My professor said their complaints weren't my fault. Kids act that way a lot because no one really likes having to wear braces. But still, having all those big complainers today was upsetting for me."

"Know what you mean," said Jelly Bean, pursing her lips together. She felt proud to be talked to like an adult. Roger-Over came by to lick up some donut crumbs from the floor. Michael and Sam's voices came closer to the house. "Oh, Uncle Jack," said Jelly Bean, jolted into remembering something important, "make Joel promise not to tell Mom I got sent to Mr. Johnston's office today. He saw me when I was on the way there. And that wasn't really my fault, either. Just like what happened to you today wasn't really your fault."

"I'll take care of him." Uncle Jack winked. He walked quietly to the door to the deck, where Michael and Sam had just come in, both of them completely out of breath. Joel was right behind them. In what seemed like a second, Joel was on the floor, pinned tightly in Uncle Jack's wrestling hold. "You weren't planning to say anything to your mother about your sister being sent to the principal's office, were you Joel?"

"No, definitely not!" he called out.

"Were you, Joel?" Uncle Jack asked again.

"Let me up!" came Joel's muffled screams.

"What happened, Jell?" asked Sam, her middle brother, throwing his jacket and cap on a chair, then grabbing a bottle of the energy drink he liked from the refrigerator.

"I got sent to Mr. Johnston's office," Jelly Bean explained. "Ms. Peiser caught me talking, but I was just trying to find out from Taylor if I got a part in the play. I got to school a little bit late today."

"Taylor been bugging you?" asked Sam, pulling a chocolate bar out of his back pocket and offering half of it to Jelly Bean.

"How did you know?" Jelly Bean asked. Sam always seemed to figure out what was bothering her, without her having to say much.

"Just had a feeling," he answered.

Roger-Over puttered over from the kitchen to the den, and scampered around to join Uncle Jack and Joel who were lying on their backs on the carpet. They were both out of breath. He nestled in between them.

Jelly Bean stayed with Sam in the kitchen. "Taylor's so mean now," Jelly Bean told him. "And she's been getting meaner."

Sam shrugged and studied his candy bar, slowly peeling the wrapper into strips. "Some people are mean, Jel, that's how it is. But you can't let them know it bothers you. It's the only way they'll stop. If you do that, they'll move on to someone else."

"Oh," said Jelly Bean, staring at Sam and mulling over what he said. She put her part of the chocolate bar on the kitchen table and carefully broke apart the six squares. "When I grow up, do you think I'll still have friends' problems?" she asked him.

"Most probably yes," said Sam. "I think everyone does." He was fifteen and had managed to figure a lot of things out.

She thought about that for a minute. "Do grownups have friends' problems?"

"Don't know," he answered. "Guessing they probably do."

They both jumped when just then a bunch of ice cubes came tumbling out of the ice-maker part of the refrigerator, and skidded all over the floor. Someone must have pressed the ice-maker and it had stuck, which Mom had warned everyone could happen. Roger-Over trotted in, chased some of the ice-cubes, then finally caught one in his paw and began crunching on it.

When Uncle Jack bent down to clean up the mess, Joel sneaked up behind him, scooped up an ice cube and put it down Uncle Jack's back. Uncle Jack got him back by bringing him down in another wrestling hold – this time on the kitchen floor. Then Sam got up and fast as lightning grabbed another ice-cube from the floor and put it down Uncle Jack's back. But Uncle Jack was quicker. He reached out one hand and grabbed Sam by the ankle. In a split second, he had Sam pinned on the floor too. Roger-Over yelped and wouldn't stop. He always loved getting in the middle of the action. He was a dog who loved fun.

No wonder Mom said she needed a rubber room in the house. Funny that Jelly Bean was thinking about Mom, because just then she heard the car door slam in the garage, and then Mom was trudging up the stairs with grocery bags, calling over the racket for someone to come help her.

"Coming," Michael called and went down to help Mom bring up the rest of the bags. Michael was in twelfth grade. He was Jelly Bean's oldest brother, and she usually didn't have too much to do with him. He was on his phone a lot, or driving around somewhere ever since he got his license. Sometimes he liked to tell Jelly Bean she was an accident, but then everyone told him in an angry way that that wasn't a nice thing to say.

"Jack Miller! How old are you?" Mom yelled when she got to the top of the stairs. It was always funny to hear Mom scold Uncle Jack. He was her younger brother. He was a lot younger than Mom.

"Just turned twelve," said Uncle Jack, not even looking up. He was still holding down the two boys, even though he was sweating and grunting a lot. Her brothers were pretty big too. Jelly Bean could barely believe how strong Uncle Jack was. He was always telling her he pumped a lot of iron in the gym downstairs in his building.

"You're acting worse than any twelve-year-old," Mom told him. "Are you waiting till someone gets hurt? Get up, right now!" Mom meant business. Uncle Jack stood up and saluted. She just shook her head, and put the bag of groceries she was holding on the kitchen counter. Uncle Jack tried to give her a kiss, but she pushed him away.

Joel and Sam got up, slowly, moaning and groaning. "Sam, please clean up that ice. It's already melting all over the floor and someone's going to slip. Joel, please go walk Roger-Over. Which reminds me – whoever was supposed to walk him this morning and forgot, may now have the pleasure of walking him every morning this week." She looked right at Joel.

"Jack," she went on, "you can set the table for dinner, and Jillian, come help me put away these groceries." That was Jelly Bean's favorite job because she got to see what Mom had bought, and she could put all the things she liked where she could easily find them. "Michael, please make the salad," she asked him. Then Mom acted like she didn't hear everyone's complaints. "Here," she said, tossing Michael three bags of chopped-up vegetables. "Just put these in a bowl and mix. Can you handle that?" Mom turned around and smiled at Michael so he'd know she was just teasing him.

"Sandy, I'm not staying for dinner," Uncle Jack told Mom.

"Oh no?" Mom answered. She took a vegetable brush out of the drawer and started scrubbing some potatoes. Wow, she did that fast, Jelly Bean noticed.

"Nope. I have to go," he told her. Uncle Jack picked up his jacket from the kitchen chair where he had tossed it.

"Going out for dinner?" asked Mom. Everyone knew that Uncle Jack never cooked anything for himself in his apartment. When they had last gone over to his apartment, all his refrigerator had in it was a carton of orange juice and some packets of mustard and ketchup. Mom put the potatoes in the oven, and took some pink slimy slabs of chicken out of the refrigerator. "Not sick of my cooking, are you?"

"Maybe." Uncle Jack was smiling. He winked at Jelly Bean.

"Maybe what?" Mom asked, turning around, just enough so she could see him.

"You know I could never get sick of your cooking," he told Mom, putting his big giant arm around her. Mom looked teeny compared to him.

"Suzanne again?" Mom asked, putting the pieces of chicken in a pan. She poured some kind of reddish-brown sauce over them. Raw meat looked disgusting. But Roger-Over was interested. Very interested. "Get away!" Mom yelled at him. He stood at attention a step or two behind her, waiting patiently in case she just happened to drop something on the floor. She didn't. Mom was pretty careful.

"Probably," Uncle Jack answered again, in a mysterious way. "Maybe I'll see you later," he said. Then he reached down and grabbed Jelly Bean, who dropped the bag of potato chips she was about to put away, as he slung her over his shoulder. "Bye for now," he called over his shoulder to Mom, and headed for the front door. Jelly Bean started screaming, and beating Uncle

26

Jack's back with her fists as he walked to the door with her upside-down, bouncing against his back. It was kind of fun, but a little scary. It was also making her a little nauseous.

"Jack Miller, put her down now!" Mom yelled to him in a loud voice. "Are you serious about her?" she asked him, taking a tomato out of the refrigerator, and giving it a shower in the sink.

"About Jillian? Of course I'm serious about my favorite niece."

"Put me down!" Jelly Bean told him again. Now she was really nauseous from being held upside-down and bounced around like crazy.

"About Suzanne," said Mom, crunching on a piece of one of the cucumbers, as she fixed the salad Michael had made a big mess of, so that now it looked pretty. She turned around and shook her head at Uncle Jack.

"Of course, I'm serious about Suzanne," Uncle Jack answered. "I'm a very serious person. You should know that by now."

Uncle Jack put Jelly Bean down, finally. But then he started making such silly faces at her – pulling out his ears, scrunching up his nose, and sticking his tongue out really far – that Jelly Bean laughed so hard she couldn't stop.

"Jack, you know what I mean." Mom said impatiently.

"Yeah, you know what she means," Sam chimed in, who had just about cleaned up the ice and melted water from the floor. But he had thrown paper towels on the garbage for recycling so high that the whole mess toppled over. Mom had to remind him for the thousandth time to start a new bag when the last one got full. Boys needed a lot of reminding.

"How about emptying the garbage?" Mom asked Uncle Jack, turning around so she faced him.

"I'll see you later," said Uncle Jack, opening the front door.

"Jack, I asked you to please take the garbage," Mom called after him, practically begging.

"Oops – I meant to, but then I forgot," said Uncle Jack. He did look like he wasn't really listening to what Mom was saying.

"If you do come by later," Mom called after him, "don't make it too late."

"How come you kept asking him if he was serious?" Jelly Bean asked Mom, after she heard Uncle Jack's car pull away. She scooped up her bag of chips and plopped down in a kitchen chair.

"I just wanted to know if he likes her a lot," Mom answered. She grabbed the bag of chips away from Jelly Bean. "Don't eat that right before dinner," she told her. Jelly Bean groaned. Mom sank down in one of the other chairs and started checking her messages.

"Oh," said Jelly Bean. It was annoying when Mom didn't want to spend much time explaining something to her. Mom did look tired. Still, it wasn't easy being the youngest. It felt like everyone else always understood what Mom meant much better than she did. Or maybe they just didn't care as much about certain things as she did. While Mom texted away, Jelly Bean went behind her and rested her elbows on Mom's shoulders.

"Ow," said Mom, turning around. "Jillian come on, that hurts." At least she had gotten Mom's attention.

The phone in the kitchen rang. Sometimes it seemed silly having land-lines in the house, when everyone now had their own phones. Besides, Mom always complained they got so many annoyance calls, and they were usually during dinner.

Sam picked it up. "It's for you," he said to Jelly Bean. "I'm going upstairs to do my homework." He hurried out of the kitchen, and hopped up the stairs two at a time.

"Come down in half an hour for dinner," Mom yelled after him.

"Mom," asked Jelly Bean, "can Heather Farrell come over this weekend?"

"I can't see why not," said Mom, pulling a nail file out of her pocketbook. "Saturday would be okay." She concentrated on filing one of her nails. "Shoot," she said. Her nail must have broken far down. "I didn't realize you two were friends."

"Mom!" said Jelly Bean, covering the receiver, "she can hear you!"

"Sorry," said Mom, but not like she really meant it.

"You could come over on Saturday Heather," Jelly Bean told her. She waited for her to answer. "Good," she said, trying to sound enthusiastic. Mom looked up from her filing. "Okay, I'll see you about twelve on Saturday," Jelly Bean said, and then paused. "I'm doing okay. Thanks Heather. See you in school tomorrow." Jelly Bean hung up. She felt miserable.

"Don't you have plans with Taylor this Saturday, Jilly?" Mom asked, getting up to check the pan of chicken in the oven. "I thought her mother told me she was taking Taylor and some friends to the movies and out for ice-cream."

"Well, I guess I'm not one of those friends," said Jelly Bean, putting her head down on her arms on the kitchen table. Her hair spread out all over the silverware and napkins, but she didn't care. "I'm a loser Mom," said Jelly Bean.

"I don't think you're a loser," said Mom. Jelly Bean turned her head and moved her hair a little so she could watch Mom cutting up some melon and putting it in a bowl. "No!" Mom snapped at Roger-Over, who was trying to gobble up a piece of melon rind that had fallen on the floor. "Oh well," she said, rolling her eyes. Roger-Over was happy to eat any kind of food – or garbage – that came his way.

"You have to say that," said Jelly Bean. "You're my mom." For a minute, Mom looked like she didn't remember what Jelly Bean was talking about. It seemed like her mind was a million other places. "Taylor's the biggest brat in the whole entire world. But she's so popular now, and she's been so mean to me. And I have no idea what I did." Jelly Bean broke into loud sobs.

Mom sat down next to Jelly Bean and stroked her hair. Then she told Jelly Bean to sit up. She smoothed her forehead, and handed her a tissue to blow her nose. Jelly Bean felt all sweaty and disgusting. She sat up. Her hair stuck up all over the place but she didn't care. She folded her arms, and slouched down in her chair.

"What a brat," said Mom. "I'm going to talk to Gale about her. Other people have been complaining about the way she's been acting too. I think I need to have a talk with Ms. Peiser." Mom got up and pulled the pan of chicken out of the oven. It smelled all tomato-y and delicious.

"No! Don't do that, Mom," said Jelly Bean, swiveling around in her chair and jumping up. Now Mom was about to figure out a way to make things even worse. Sometimes she had some good ideas, but this one was terrible. She probably shouldn't have said anything to her about Taylor.

"All right," Mom sighed. "If you really don't want me to, I won't."

Mom pursed her lips together. Then she got up and finished fixing the table for dinner. "Try not paying attention to her at all for the next few days and see what happens. I bet she'll start acting nicer to you after that. That's the way it usually works." Maybe, thought Jelly Bean. But she thought about Shelby Trankman and her group of popular girls. None of them would care at all if Jelly Bean ignored them. They wouldn't even notice. But it wouldn't do any good trying to explain all that to Mom. She always said she had been through the same kinds of problems when she was younger, but Jelly Bean didn't see how anything could have been this bad.

"I'm not going to get a good part in the play either," Jelly Bean told Mom, as she got up to put a few ice cubes in each person's glass.

"Sorry to hear that, Jilly," said Mom. "I know how much you wanted one." She gave Jelly Bean a quick hug. "Sometimes everything goes wrong. That goes for grownups too." Mom poured water in each glass.

"Anyway, Ms. Peiser said she's going to tell me tomorrow whether I might be able to get a speaking part. But she doubts it. She never got your message, either," Jelly Bean added.

"Well," said Mom, reaching over to grab her phone off the edge of the countertop, and looking like she really didn't feel like listening to any more complaints right now, "try not to get too upset over that kind of thing. There'll be other plays. Don't forget, you still have gymnastics, and maybe it's better not to have too much else besides homework taking up all your free time. You know how Grandma always says kids need time just to have fun."

"I know, I know," said Jelly Bean. "All you ever used to do after school was play out on the street with the other kids in the neighborhood." Mom loved repeating that. Jelly Bean leaned down and snuggled up close to Roger-Over, who had come padding over to her. Jelly Bean nuzzled his nose with hers.

"Jillian," said Mom, sounding worn out, "how many times do I have to tell you not to do that? You see what he sticks his nose into in the yard."

"I'm just upset," Jelly Bean explained. "I'm not thinking clearly." She squeezed Roger-Over really hard. "You're so cute," she told him.

"Oh boy," said Mom, shaking her head. She put the salad bowl in the middle of the table.

"Do you know what my parents used to say to me?" Mom asked. Jelly Bean groaned. "Expect to be blessed. That's what our old pastor used to say. The one we had when I was growing up."

"That doesn't help, Mom," Jelly Bean groaned. She flipped over and lay her head on Roger-Over, as if he were a pillow. But he shook himself and shuffled away, closer to Mom and the food.

Mom turned around and put her hands on her hips. "How about calling your brothers down for dinner?"

Jelly Bean called each one of them loudly. "That's another thing, Ma," said Jelly Bean, "you know they never listen to me."

Mom called them and down they came. "Guess what?" Mom asked Jelly Bean.

"What?" said Jelly Bean, feeling gloomy as a raincloud.

"It's always darkest before the dawn," said Mom.

"Oh boy," said Jelly Bean. "What's that supposed to mean?" She flipped over and began carefully inspecting Roger-Over's ears.

"It means that just when things can't get any worse, that's when everything starts looking up." Mom inspected her nails. "Besides, tomorrow's Friday. That ought to make you happy. Now please get up off the floor, and leave that poor dog alone."

Jelly Bean heard Dad's key in the front door. "Daddy!" she called, flying to him like a bullet and almost knocking him over. At least he pretended to almost be knocked over. Dad gave Mom a kiss over Jelly Bean's head, put his briefcase down and crouched down to give Jelly Bean a big hug.

"How are my favorite girls?" he asked.

"Pretty good Bill." Mom answered, looking up at him. "How about you? How was your day?"

Jelly Bean grabbed on to Dad's arm as he started answering Mom, and they all walked into the kitchen. She wanted to tell Dad all about what had happened at school that day, but just then Michael, Sam and Joel came tumbling down the stairs. They were always so loud, interrupting her all the time, and talking right over her. They were always laughing, joking or arguing with each other, using their elbows to shove each other out of the way. They did talk to her during dinner – when they needed her to pass something.

It felt like her brothers hogged all of Mom and Dad's attention, telling them about games and practices and tests that were coming up, who did or said some stupid thing, and what they needed money for. A few times Joel told Jelly Bean how dumb she was when she tried to say something. Michael shushed her when he was in the middle of a story. Sam was the only one who smiled and winked at her from time to time during dinner, and Jelly Bean knew she could count on him to explain whatever she didn't understand later.

After dinner Jelly Bean was sitting in the den with Mom and Dad, when the doorbell rang. Dad got up to open the door, and in walked Uncle Jack and Suzanne. Suzanne, who Uncle Jack had been mentioning a lot lately. Suzanne, who had long, thick blond hair, a fancy white coat with a furry collar, and long legs that ended in shiny tall black heels. Suzanne, who looked like the fairy princess in the stories Mom and Dad used to read to Jelly Bean when she was little.

"Where are you two off to?" Mom asked, after everyone said hello. Jelly Bean almost didn't recognize Uncle Jack. His hair was all shiny and slicked back, and he was wearing a long tan coat instead of one of the beat-up sports jackets he usually wore. He looked like he was standing up very straight and tall, and he smelled like he had put on a lot of men's perfume. He didn't seem at all like the same person who had been wrestling with the boys and twirling her around in the air just a little while ago. Jelly Bean kept staring at him, but it seemed like that was okay, because everyone else was staring too. Except everyone was mostly staring at Suzanne. It looked like two movie stars had walked into their living room. And the living room was a big mess.

"We're going to the Red Rooster," said Uncle Jack. He looked over at Suzanne and smiled.

"Wow!" said Michael, Sam and Joel at the same time. It looked like none of them knew what to do with their arms. Sam folded his. Michael whistled. The Red Rooster was the fanciest restaurant around, everyone knew that. The boys kept shifting from side to side and continued staring at Suzanne. They didn't have much else to say. They did knock into each other a few times though, and then each one told the other to stop.

"No, you stop," Joel said to Michael, and tried to jam his elbow into Michael's side, but Michael caught his elbow and laughed.

"Stop it, everyone," Mom hissed.

"It's a special night for us," said Uncle Jack, after he cleared his throat. Suzanne whispered something to him. Jelly Bean wondered if everyone else except her knew what was going on. "Jelly Bean," Uncle Jack crouched down and said to her softly, "would you take Suzanne up to your room for a minute?"

Up they went. Why would Suzanne need to go to her room? Did she need to lie down? Borrow something? Change her clothes? If she needed to go to the bathroom, she could have gone to the downstairs one – even though it could have been a big mess, and Uncle Jack might have figured that out. Did she have a gift for her? Not likely. None of her guesses turned out to be right.

"Do you have a strong light I could put next to this mirror, just for now?" Suzanne asked, once they were in Jelly Bean's room.

"How about this one?" Jelly Bean pointed to the one on her desk that she used for doing homework.

"That'll work," said Suzanne, throwing her coat on the bed. Next, she kicked off her shiny black high heels.   Roger-Over barked at her, and Jelly

Bean had to hold him back when it looked like he might be thinking about biting her. Suzanne turned her pocketbook on its side, gave it a shake, and out spilled tiny jars, tubes and small bottles, until Jelly Bean's desk was covered in make-up. Suzanne went like wildfire, shaking and dipping brushes everywhere, rubbing and smudging powder and cream all over her face, and penciling in lines over her eyes and her lips. "I didn't get a chance to do my make-up today," she told Jelly Bean, who just sat on the edge of her bed, listening and staring and then running around getting Suzanne the things she asked for – like tissues and cotton balls and a cup of water, and even one of Mom's tweezers. "I got out of work late, and then just as soon as I got home, I barely had time to take a shower and change before Jack picked me up." She went on and on. Then suddenly Suzanne stood up, fixed her really tight black skirt where it was all crumpled up, and pulled her blouse down lower in front so that a lot more of her skin was showing above the top button.

Jelly Bean had not ever seen anything like this in her whole life, even in a movie that was really meant for older teenagers or grownups. "What time is it?" Suzanne asked, in a worried way. "I don't want to miss our reservation, but I can't go anywhere without my make-up on. I had a problem with my lenses at work today, and I look awful when I wear my glasses. I'll just have to be blind tonight."

"Really blind?" asked Jelly Bean.

"Well not as in totally blind, but I just won't be able to see so well. Jack'll have to read me the menu. Hope I can see what I'm eating!"

Jelly Bean laughed. Suzanne must have seen her eyeing the pack of cigarettes that had fallen out of her pocketbook along with her ton of make-up. "I know, I know, I still smoke," she said. Jelly Bean blushed. She didn't know what to say. "How else am I supposed to stay thin?" Suzanne asked.

"It's really bad for you," Jelly Bean said, finally. Suzanne gave her an annoyed look, then started throwing all the make-up back in her bag.

"Nosy," Jelly Bean heard Suzanne mutter under her breath. Jelly Bean sat cross-legged on her bed and watched. Roger-Over started barking at Suzanne again, and no matter what Jelly Bean tried saying or doing to get him to stop, he wouldn't.

Suzanne mumbled something else under her breath. It sounded like she couldn't believe she was being lectured by a ten-year-old.

"I have to get going," Suzanne said, fixing her blouse one more time and smoothing her skirt. She stood in front of Jelly Bean's mirror for a minute and put a tissue between her lips and bit down. Her lips were bright red. "How do I look?" she asked Jelly Bean, turning from side to side and not taking her eyes off the mirror.

"Fine," said Jelly Bean, and gave her as nice a smile as she could manage. Suzanne took one long last look in the mirror and then grabbed her coat off the bed. Jelly Bean noticed that when she leaned over, her blouse went down really low. She couldn't stop staring.

"Can you do me a favor?" Suzanne asked. "Pull down my skirt a little in the back?" Jelly Bean did. "That's enough!" she said, pushing Jelly Bean's hand away. "It keeps bunching up."

"Are you serious with my uncle?" Jelly Bean blurted out, bouncing up and down on her bed, and then felt herself turning bright red. But it had just come out.

"Oooooh!" Suzanne laughed, but her laugh sounded fake. Her hand was on the doorknob. "What a funny question from a little squirt like you!" She stopped in the middle of opening the door. Jelly Bean knew her face was as red as Suzanne's lipstick. "Why do you ask?"

"I don't know," said Jelly Bean. "I was just wondering."

She couldn't pry her eyes off this person who looked so strange in her room. What if Uncle Jack got mad at her when he found out what she had asked Suzanne? What a disaster. Why did she have to blurt that out? Jelly Bean wished she could go back and press "delete." And anyway, why did Suzanne have to put her make-up on in *her* room? Just when she thought things couldn't get any worse, they had managed to. Jelly Bean felt dumber right now than she had ever felt in her entire life.

"Jack told me everyone calls you Jelly Bean," Suzanne said, giving her a funny look. "Why is that?" she asked, in a not very nice tone, while they walked downstairs. She didn't feel like walking with Suzanne, but it didn't seem as if she had a choice.

"My real name's Jillian Bonnie," Jelly Bean answered. "Everyone just started calling me Jelly Bean when I was little. Well, almost everyone."

"Oh," said Suzanne, as if she wasn't really too interested. She checked her phone when they were halfway down the stairs. Her clothes rustled as Jelly Bean followed her down.

"You ready honey?" Suzanne asked Uncle Jack when she was back standing next to him in the living room, and they were holding hands. Uncle Jack had an odd look on his face, one Jelly Bean didn't think she had ever seen before. Then something strange happened. Uncle Jack got down on one knee, opened a little black box he was holding, and showed Suzanne a bright sparkly ring. He said it was for her. Sam whispered to Jelly Bean that meant they were engaged. Mom had tears in her eyes. She hugged Suzanne. So did Dad. It didn't look like she was hugging back too much, but maybe she wasn't much of a hugger. Or maybe she just didn't want to get her make-up and clothes messed up. Everyone said congratulations to both of them, so Jelly Bean did too. Dad and the boys smacked Uncle Jack on his back, and then each one gave him a hug all over again. Jelly Bean stood in between Mom and Dad, and kept looking away from Uncle Jack. When she finally forced herself to look at him, he was smiling away.

Chapter 3

In Which the Only One Who Seems Interested What Jelly Bean Has to Say Is Her Beloved Dog Roger-Over

After Uncle Jack and Suzanne left, the boys went up to their rooms, which left Jelly Bean downstairs with Mom and Dad all to herself. That was good, because there were a few things she needed to have cleared up.

"Jillian, guess what?" said Mom before Jelly Bean had a chance to say anything, "You're going to be a flower girl in Uncle Jack's wedding!" What about this would this make Mom so excited? Couldn't she see how strange the person was that Uncle Jack was marrying? Couldn't anyone tell? She needed to alert everyone, but who would listen? Probably no one. And if anyone did listen to her, who would believe her? It was a lost cause.

"Great," said Jelly Bean, plopping down on the couch next to Mom. She knew she should be getting ready for bed, but it was going to be impossible to calm down after all that drama.

"Wonder when they're going to get married, Sandy?" Dad said. He turned on the tv and started watching a football game that was on.   Dad looked like he didn't really want to think about Uncle Jack's wedding either, but it did seem like he was trying hard to say things that would make Mom happy.

"I don't really like Suzanne," said Jelly Bean. "In my room she was acting weird."

"I have no idea," Mom answered Dad, ignoring her remark. It figured. "Jillian, I'm not sure why you'd say something like that," Mom finally responded to her. "We hardly even know Suzanne." Jelly Bean debated with herself about telling Mom and Dad more details of how Suzanne had acted in her room. She decided not to. Mom wanted to be excited about Uncle Jack's wedding, and that was that. "They'll probably make it right after Jack's graduation, would be my best guess," said Mom. After that, Mom was off and running. "Well Jillian, you're going to have a new aunt! It'll all be so exciting. You'll see."

Sounds awful, thought Jelly Bean.

Dad looked like he was in his own world, clicking away with the remote, going from channel to channel. Dad hated commercials. It was enough to make Jelly Bean dizzy, watching the tv screen. Mom wanted someone to be excited with – badly. So naturally she called Grandma.

"Woohoo," Jelly Bean answered, hoping either Mom or Dad would notice her frown. Neither one did – or if they did see it, they were purposely not paying attention. Dad patted her back and settled in to watch some news show. He probably needed to watch something boring after all that commotion.

"Ma?" Jelly Bean heard Mom in the kitchen, chattering away to Grandma. "Did he tell you?" Grandma must have said no. "It did happen pretty fast," Mom was saying. "I guess they must have known from the time they met." Grandma must have asked her for more details, because Mom started telling her all about what had just happened.

Suddenly Roger-Over yelped. Mom must have stepped on either his foot or his tail while she was talking to Grandma. "Oops, sorry Roge," she said. Then Roger-Over did something Jelly Bean had ever seen him do before. First, he started barking really loud. Then he got a running start in the kitchen, ran through the den to where Dad was sitting, and jumped way up so that he landed right smack in the middle of Dad's lap. Even he was acting a little crazy listening to Mom talk about Uncle Jack marrying Suzanne.

"Whoa there, boy!" said Dad. He was so startled that he sat straight up, and his glasses came tumbling down onto Roger-Over. Jelly Bean giggled. She ran over and hugged Dad and Roger-Over. Then she pushed Roger-Over off Dad's lap and sat on it herself. He shook himself and settled at Dad's feet.

"Do you like Suzanne?" Jelly Bean asked Dad, turning around and slinging her arms around his neck. She leaned her head against his chest. Mom was still in the kitchen on the phone, talking to Grandma a mile a minute.

"She seems nice," said Dad, putting his arm around her. With his free hand, he worked on the crossword puzzle he had just started. "You don't think so, Jilly?" said Dad, looking down at the puzzle. "You might just need to get used to her," he added absently. "It can take a little time." He switched back to watching the game.

"Well, I don't like her at all," she told Dad. "And I could never get used to her. She's a kid-hater, I could tell. And anyway, how did Uncle Jack find her, Dad?" She slid off Dad's lap and kneeled on the rug, so she could pet Roger-Over, who had flipped over on his back with his paws in the air. He was the best dog in the world.

"You'd have to ask Mom, Jilly. I have no idea."

Jelly Bean spent a few minutes carefully inspecting one of Roger-Over's ears. He looked up at her with droopy eyes. She could tell he understood what she was unhappy about.

"I think I need to warn Uncle Jack," Jelly Bean told Dad, switching to checking Roger-Over's feet. He didn't like that at all, so he got up and wandered over to a different spot on the rug where he must have figured he wouldn't be bothered.

"Give her a chance, Jilly," said Dad. "You only just met her today. One day you'll be the new person in someone else's family," he said, picking up the newspaper with his crossword puzzle in it, and starting to work on it again. "You wouldn't want everyone in that person's family making up their minds they don't like you right after they've just met you for the first time." He looked over at her and smiled.

"I guess," said Jelly Bean, getting up to practice the splits. That was too far away and strange to think about. All she really felt like doing was moping. It was terrible not to be understood. Then Dad had to answer his phone. Suddenly he sounded full of energy, so Jelly Bean guessed it was probably someone from work. Mom always said how much Dad's clients loved him. Jelly Bean wandered over to the kitchen to stand by Mom, where she was still talking to Grandma. She tugged on Mom's pants leg, even though she knew that was babyish and was only going to make Mom mad. Roger-Over marched over to where Jelly Bean was standing, and he looked so cute she had to start running so he would follow her. Dogs were so much more fun than people. Jelly Bean and Roger-Over chased each other around and around in a circle through the kitchen, dining room and den. Jelly Bean started singing a song she had heard on "America's Got Talent," and Roger-Over barked along. He couldn't sing, but he sure tried.

"Jillian," said Mom, covering the phone, "do you have any homework to finish up? What on earth are you trying to do? Ma, I'm not sure what's the matter with her," she said into the phone in a loud whisper. "She's having a very strange reaction to Jack getting engaged." Then Mom turned to Jelly Bean and said, "You better go up and take a bath and get ready for bed. It's 8:30 already." She went back to talking to Grandma. Jelly Bean wondered whether Mom was not going to be able to concentrate on anything else until Uncle Jack's wedding was over with.

"Oh yeah, you have to sign some of my homework," Jelly Bean told her. She went upstairs to bring down some homework papers, found a pen and handed them both to Mom. Mom scribbled her name where Jelly Bean pointed, but she was barely paying attention. She was still going on a mile a minute about this wedding business.

"Come on, Roge," Jelly Bean sighed. "Let's go up." She snapped her fingers in front of him. "You're the only one who's never too busy for me," Jelly Bean told him when they had trudged upstairs and she was sprawled out on her bed. She held out her hand and Roger-Over licked it. He handed her his paw. "You never get sick of doing that, do you?" she asked him. He just looked up at her with his understanding eyes. She was positive he was smiling, in a doggie kind of way.

Talking to Roger-Over always cheered her up. "Everything went wrong today Roge, and I mean everything," she told him, leaning over on her side to reach down and give him a tummy rub. "I doubt I'm going to get a decent part in the play. All because I came late to school after I managed to fall into the toilet. And that's about the only part of school I was looking forward to." Roger-Over tilted his head to one side, and stared up at her. Jelly Bean gave him the bone she had hidden way under her bed, because he deserved it. He was such a good listener.

"Then," she went on, "my best friend – or, anyway, the person who's supposed to be my best friend – is so mean to me that now it's not even funny. Seriously, Roge. I don't understand what made Taylor change all of a sudden. She's been getting other kids to be mean to me too. And not just any old kids. The popular kids – you know, the ones who really count. It's like you can't get to be popular without being mean to someone else. So I really have no friends at all right now. This sucks, Roge. Most of the time my stomach feels tight as a knot. I could hardly eat lunch today, and I could barely eat anything for dinner, either. I don't feel like going to school tomorrow at all, but I know Mom will make me go. And, well, I don't want to be a quitter." She sighed. Jelly Bean figured Roger-Over didn't understand everything she had told him, but he did know for sure that she was upset. He pushed his head underneath her arm. "Hey, that tickles," she told him. And she could tell he was trying to cheer her up.

"At least Heather Farrell's been nice to me," she told him, scratching his head. "I never paid any attention to her before. She is kind of babyish, but I need to have someone to be friends with. I wonder why some people are nice and some are so mean," she asked him. Roger-Over yawned. It was such a big yawn that his jaw made a loud clicking sound. Then he rested his chin on his bone, like it was a pillow. He was a funny dog.

"And now," Jelly Bean went on, "on top of everything, Uncle Jack is getting married. He's one of my favorite people in the whole wide world, Roge. And I don't like Suzanne. That's who he's marrying. She's awful. She's as beautiful as a fairy princess, but she acts like she doesn't care about anyone except herself." Jelly Bean leaned back and put her arms behind her head. "She definitely didn't like me very much. I bet Uncle Jack's not going to be hanging around here too much anymore. We always have so much fun together, flying kites, playing monopoly, going out for breakfast, just goofing around. Just about everything Mom and Dad always say they want to do with me, but never get around to. Or maybe they just forget. I know they're busy with work and driving everybody around and all kinds of other stuff. And now I won't be able to have fun with Uncle Jack anymore either. I can tell. So just about everything's going wrong."

The next thing she knew, Mom was gently shaking her awake. "Jillian! You fell asleep in your clothes!" Mom and Dad were both standing over her when Jelly Bean yawned and opened first one eye and then the other.

"I don't give a hoot," Jelly Bean told them, and turned over. Someone she had overheard in the school office had used that expression earlier today – or was it still today? Then Mom said Roger-Over could stay in her room, but that he did need to go out one last time. Meantime Jelly Bean saw Mom fumbling around in her dresser drawers, trying to find pajamas for her to wear and complaining to Dad that it was so messy in there no one could find a blessed thing.

"Do I really have to change, Ma?" Jelly Bean asked. "I'm too tired to do anything."

"I'll help you change honey," said Mom, starting to help Jelly Bean get out of her clothes. "How about getting washed up?"

40

"Ugh, who feels like it," said Jelly Bean, scampering back into bed once she was changed. "I'll do it in the morning," she told Mom, even though she had gotten all sweaty earlier, which didn't feel good at all.

"Come on Jilly," said Mom. "You're always kissing and hugging that dog. Let me help you and we can do it quickly."

"His name's Roger-Over," said Jelly Bean. "I need him back in here as soon as possible. He's the only one who gives me the time of day." Mom just shook her head and finally talked Jelly Bean into at least brushing her teeth. When she was done, it did feel good to scamper back to her room and dive under the covers.

"What's the matter?" Jelly Bean asked Dad at breakfast the next day. It took him a while to look up.

"Oh," Dad said finally, in a tired voice, "a lot of people lost a lot of money, and they're trying to get at least some of it back," he told her.

Mom brought her coffee cup to the table, and started scratching Dad's back. Coffee smelled so good; funny how it tasted so awful.

"How did they lose a lot of money, Dad?" Jelly Bean asked.

"They believed someone who promised them he'd make them a lot of money if they gave him some of their money," Dad explained.

Jelly Bean picked apart a tangerine, and tried hard to understand what Dad had said. "That's dumb," she said, finally, "why would anyone believe someone who promised them that?"

"It happens all the time Jilly," Dad answered, as Jelly Bean ate her tangerine slowly, slice by juicy slice, and tried hard to understand. "People like to take risks," said Dad. It all kept making less and less sense.

"Then those people are dumb," said Jelly Bean. "I'd never do something like that." Dad smiled at her and patted her hand. She was so glad she could make him smile, she felt like she might burst.

"Earth to Jillian," Mom was saying to her, as she tried to juggle two more tangerines, while she was deciding whether or not to have a piece of toast. "Honey you need to finish up and get your things together."

Then the boys clattered downstairs, and Jelly Bean and her groaning got lost in the shuffle.

Chapter 4

The Play, Trying to Find Someone to Sit with at Lunch,
and Becoming Friends with Britney

The first thing Ms. Peiser did when she walked into class was call Jelly Bean up to her desk. "I've decided on an interesting part for you in the play, Jillian," she told her, "since I know how much you want to be on stage."

Jelly Bean began to perk up. "When the pilgrims land at Plymouth Rock," Ms. Peiser went on, "they'll be standing outdoors during the whole scene. Since we'll want it to look like they're really outside, and they'll be standing right near their ship, I'd like you to be in charge of rocking the ship back and forth throughout the entire first act. At first, I was thinking of setting up a fan next to the ship, but I think this is going to look more authentic. You know that the ship is going to be made out of a large piece of cardboard. I've decided to set it up so that it can be rocked back and forth by someone pushing a piece of cardboard attached to the back of the ship. So Jillian, I'd like you to stand behind the ship, dressed to look like a tree, and push the ship back and forth a little from time to time. This way it'll look like it's anchored right next to the land."

Could this really be happening? Was this a joke? One of those dreams that made no sense? Was this Ms. Peiser's way of teasing her? Michael and Joel loved saying stupid things she believed, and then laughed like crazy when they told her they were just kidding. This did not seem to be any kind of a joke, though. Ms. Peiser didn't start laughing, or saying she was just kidding. "But Ms. Peiser," Jelly Bean finally forced herself to answer, "I don't think I can find a good tree costume."

"I've given that some thought also," said Ms. Peiser, "and it's easier than you think. All you need are dark leggings and a long top. That and a few large green leaves, which you can easily make out of cardboard during art, and they can attach to your back and to a brown headband. You think you can manage that? Good then," said Ms. Peiser. And before Jelly Bean could blink, she had turned to talk to the next person waiting in line. Jelly Bean suddenly felt invisible.

"Yes, Reese, what is it dear?" Ms. Peiser was saying, completely ignoring Jelly Bean's pathetic expression. Her lips felt dry all of a sudden, and she just kept standing by Ms. Peiser's desk, staring at her. She felt like she was frozen to the spot, and all she could do was try hard to think of something – anything – she could come up with to save herself from having the dumbest part in the play. Finally, Ms. Peiser gave her a look that said as plain as could be, "now you're in the way." Jelly Bean went to the back of the room to hang up her jacket, thinking about how mean some teachers were.

"Hi Jelly Bean!" Heather's voice rang out, just as Ms. Peiser was telling everyone they had to get to their seats because she needed to take attendance, they had a lot to do that morning, and they had to get started.

"Oh hi, Heather," said Jelly Bean. "Do you want to make Halloween costumes at my house when you come over?" Mom had made that suggestion in the morning before Jelly Bean left for school, and it sounded like fun. Halloween was just a week away, and Jelly Bean had no idea what to do for a costume.

"Okay, sure," Heather answered, not sounding too happy, "but could we also—"

"Whoever is not in their seats by the time I count to three," now Ms. Peiser's voice was loud and mad, "will be marked absent, and will have to go down to the office for a late pass. One, two—" Along with all the other stragglers, Jelly Bean and Heather scrambled to their seats.

At lunch, Jelly Bean didn't even try to sit at her old table. She didn't feel as bad as she had the day before, but she did have that same old knot in her stomach. It was smaller now though, so at least today she could eat.

Just then Taylor walked past with her tray, and pushed Jelly Bean's chair way over to one side. Since Jelly Bean had been sitting with one leg crossed underneath the other, she lost her balance and fell on the floor. "Ow!" she cried out, not so much because she was hurt, but because it was a surprise all of a sudden to be on the floor. She looked up and saw her soup all over Colton's lap and his book. "Oops," said Jelly Bean, and burst out laughing. Everyone else was laughing too, except Colton and Heather. But Jelly Bean knew she was laughing to cover up how embarrassed she felt.

Something even more surprising happened after that. Jelly Bean turned around to look at her old table. Everyone there was laughing, except for Shelby, who was flipping through one of her magazines. She looked bored. Taylor kept poking Shelby, trying to make her turn around to see what she had done. Shelby finally did turn around, but she didn't look like she thought anything was funny. Jelly Bean noticed, though, that she gave Taylor an annoyed look and moved her chair further away.

"You bug me once more," Shelby said loudly to Taylor, "and I'm telling Ms. Peiser." She gave Taylor a disgusted look. "Now leave me alone," she snapped. "You're getting on my nerves."

"Ms. Alpert," Ms. Peiser's voice rang out, "you can pick yourself up and step over to my table." One of the other teachers was pointing to Taylor, and it looked like she had just finished telling her what had happened. Ms. Peiser looked boiling mad.

"Jelly Bean," Heather asked, as soon as Jelly Bean sat back down with a new lunch, "would it be okay if I brought my dolls with me to your house tomorrow?"

"You said we could make Halloween costumes Heather," Jelly Bean answered, biting into her grilled cheese sandwich. She felt like telling Heather to just forget coming over, but she couldn't think of a good excuse fast enough.

"Do you think we could also have some time to play with my dolls? On Saturday and Sunday, I usually take extra special care of them. They'd probably be hurt if I ignored them this weekend." Heather's clothes always looked a few sizes too small. Her round pudgy face was surrounded by frizzy brown hair. Jelly Bean noticed she looked like one of the dolls at their table. "Do you think you could come to my house instead, then?" asked Heather.

"I can't Heather," Jelly Bean heard herself saying. "My mom told me I have to be home," she quickly added, even though she noticed Heather was giving her a funny look. Being stuck at Heather's house sounded awful. "She wants to be sure I get plenty of fresh air and exercise on the weekend, especially since I quit soccer." Jelly Bean took another bite of her sandwich. She snuck a look at Heather, who was frowning. "She keeps saying I'm spending too much time on the computer and watching TV." That wasn't exactly a lie. Mom had said she was spending much too much time inside. Just the part about not being allowed to go to someone else's house wasn't exactly what Mom had said.

"Can I bring my dolls over then?" Heather asked. "They could watch us play outside, and then watch us make Halloween costumes. I know they'd like to come with me to your house, and maybe we'd get a little chance to play with them after all." Heather sat there stroking her doll's hair. Some of the other girls at the table were making their dolls talk to one another.

Jelly Bean wondered what she had gotten herself into. Not only did she not care about dolls, but if her brothers saw her playing with them, they'd tease her about it forever. Maybe not Sam, but Michael and Joel would for sure. "Maybe we could play with your dolls a different time, Heather," Jelly Bean suggested. "Maybe another time when I can go over your house."

Heather didn't answer. Then she made her Baby Goody doll play with the other dolls at the table the whole rest of lunch period. Jelly Bean picked at the food on her plate and stared straight down, wondering if these were the only friends she'd ever have for the whole rest of the year. They weren't really her friends, anyway. She couldn't think of anything to say to any of them. She wished she could reach into her pocketbook and text someone – anyone, even Mom or Dad or Sam – but the rules about not texting during school were strict. If a teacher saw you, they could swoop down on you from out of nowhere and take away your phone. It had already happened a few times that year.

Jelly Bean was stuck: the girls she wanted to be friends with didn't want to be her friends, and the girls who wanted to be her friends acted like four-year-olds. And even some of them weren't too friendly.

That afternoon, Jelly Bean didn't have to ride home with Taylor. On Fridays she walked over to the Y for gymnastics.

Jelly Bean had never liked gymnastics all that much, but today Mrs. Clare, the instructor, complimented her and asked her to demonstrate for the rest of the class the correct way to do some of the flips and other routines.

"Are you going to States, Jelly Bean?" one of the girls asked her at the end of class.

"You're amazing," said another.

"You should be in the Olympics," said one of the others. "I bet you'd make it too."

"Watch me, Jillian," asked another. "Is this right?" one of the girls asked. Poor Jordyn! She was very tall for a fourth-grader and a little clumsy. She looked like she might be better at basketball than gymnastics. Still, she tried one of the routines they had been learning that involved a lot of cartwheels in a row. She ended up tripping over her own feet, and fell on the mat smack on her rear-end, with her feet spread apart. But she threw her head back and sat there laughing. Everyone joined in.   Wow, thought Jelly Bean – how great that this girl was able to laugh at herself instead of getting upset and giving up.

"You should watch how Jillian does it next time," said one of the other girls. Mrs. Clare went over to Jordyn to make sure she wasn't hurt.

"Everyone at school calls her Jelly Bean," Britney Keller spoke up. Britney was the only person from school who took Jelly Bean's same level gymnastics on the same day and at the same time that she did.

"Do you practice a lot at home?" Britney asked Jelly Bean, when they went into the locker room to change. They had never talked to each other before. Jelly Bean was glad Britney was turning out to be friendly. She never had been before.

"Sometimes I do," said Jelly Bean. She and Britney looked at each other. "I don't know why I said that," Jelly Bean blurted out. "I never really feel like practicing." Something made her want to be honest with Britney, even though they didn't really know each other at all. "I mean sometimes I fool around and do some handstands or cartwheels, just for fun."

"Me too," said Britney. "It relieves stress," she added.

Britney was Shelby's favorite friend now. She seemed so grown-up for a fourth-grader.

"If my brothers saw me practicing, they'd probably make fun of me. Two of them would, anyway. But sometimes I just do some cartwheels and forward and backward rolls in my room, with the door shut."

"You're really good," said Britney. "You should get a lock to put on your door. Then you'd be sure to have privacy. I wouldn't want anybody laughing at me. My mother put a lock on my door. But that was so my father couldn't burst in on me all the time."

"Really?" Jelly Bean was surprised that someone her age would need a lock on her door to keep her own dad out of her room.

"Yeah," Britney went on. "When my parents were going through their divorce, my father was behaving like an idiot. He was always bothering me, and also telling me to come live with him. He's also really physical, like when he got mad when I said I didn't want to." Britney looked at the floor. She just stood there chewing her lip.

"Oh," said Jelly Bean, not sure what to say. "What do you mean by 'physical'," she asked, finally, not sure whether or not that was a good idea to ask.

"He's a hitter," said Britney, when she finally looked up. Her eyes were wet, but only a little. "My father's insane, that's all. That's how my mom explains it. He needs meds. But he doesn't like to take them."

Britney rolled up her gymnastics clothes and stuffed them into her gym bag. Everyone else had gone upstairs. Near them it sounded like some people had said good-bye, but Jelly Bean was concentrating so hard on what Britney was saying, that what other people were saying sounded faraway. "You're a good listener," said Britney. "You know that?"

"Thanks," said Jelly Bean. "Did your dad ever hit you?" she asked, after a minute.

"Sure," said Britney. "And he hit my mom, and my sister. That's what a hitter does. That's why we can't have him around anymore."

Jelly Bean looked at Britney and tried to make sense out of what she had just told her. "But if he wanted you to come live with him so badly, why did he hit you? I wouldn't want to live with someone who hit me. Even if he was my dad."

"My dad's just plain nuts, that's all," said Britney. "He doesn't think like a normal person, that's what my mom says.

"She says he gets so mad when he thinks someone doesn't like him, he just loses his temper. He can't help it." They walked to the water fountain. "A lot of men hit," she said. "And some of them do worse things. Just watch the news any night."

"That's scary," said Jelly Bean, thinking what she'd ever do if this was happening to her.

"He always apologized afterwards," said Britney. She took a long drink from the fountain. "And then he expected us to forgive him. But finally, my mom got sick of his craziness."

"Yikes," said Jelly Bean, bending down to tie her sneakers. She felt like she was in the middle of another one of her dreams that didn't make any sense. It was hard to believe Britney was talking about her own dad.

"At least when my dad was trying to get me to stay with him, he paid for my gymnastics. He knew how badly I wanted to go," said Britney. "Now my mom's trying to work extra shifts to pay for it for me," she said.

Jelly Bean realized she was staring at Britney, trying to think of something to say. "I hope you get to keep going," she said, finally.

"Well, see you Monday," said Britney. Then before she turned to leave, she gave Jelly Bean a little smile. "I can't tell a lot of kids about all this," she said. "I feel like you care." She pushed open the heavy door, and they both walked out into the cold.

"Bye," said Jelly Bean. "See you Monday, Britney." Britney had already turned to walk in the opposite direction from the way Jelly Bean had to go. The air smelled like wet leaves, and like winter was just around the corner.

Chapter 5

In Which Jelly Bean Has Trouble Getting Along with Joel,
and a Crazy Dinner

"Hi Mom," said Jelly Bean, when she got inside the car.

Mom leaned over and gave her a kiss. Joel was in the backseat. He kicked the back of Jelly Bean's seat a few times, until she turned around. "Hi creep," she greeted him. He made a face at her, and then shook his head and went back to texting someone and laughing out loud. He was being even more annoying than usual. And he smelled all sweaty and gross too.

"Hi honey," said Mom. "Why isn't your jacket zipped all the way up? It's freezing out." Mom leaned over to start zipping up Jelly Bean's jacket.

"Mom, what are you doing? I'm in the car already, and it's really warm in here." Jelly Bean moved away from Mom.

"I know, you're right," said Mom. "I'm sorry. I guess I'm just nervous. Grandma and Grandpa, Uncle Jack and Suzanne, and Suzanne's parents are all coming over for dinner. In fact, I need to go pick up some of the special bread and rolls everyone likes." Ugh, now the ride home was going to be even longer.

"How come just Grandma and Grandpa can't come over? Why do those other people have to come too?" Jelly Bean folded her arms. "Why can't things go back to the way they were?" she whined. She heard Joel snickering in the backseat.

"Mom make him stop," said Jelly Bean. Mom turned around and gave Joel a look. It didn't do any good. He kept laughing.

"It's, well, it's traditional," said Mom, finally, honking at some other driver in front of them. "It's nice to have the people over who are going to be part of your family. Grandma and Grandpa would have had them, but you know their apartment is small, and this way they don't have to do all the cooking and cleaning up. Grandma would have loved to do all that, back in the day. This way they can just visit with Suzanne's parents. You know it's different now since Grandpa had his heart attack." Mom's voice sounded a little sad. "Too bad it took Uncle Jack so long to find someone he wants to marry."

"But how come he had to find *her*, Mom?" Jelly Bean asked.

Joel started laughing so hard he couldn't stop. Then he was out of breath, but still kept hitting his knee with his hand.

"You shut up!" Jelly Bean turned around and gave Joel her meanest look.

"Dumb," he said, shaking his head and looking out the window. But when she tried to turn around to smack him, that's when Mom pulled over.

"That's it, you two. You can either learn to behave, or there are going to be consequences. I mean it." Mom did sound like she meant it. Jelly Bean hated making Mom so mad, but when it came to Joel, that's what always seemed to happen. "And I'm sure I don't need to tell both of you to behave yourselves tonight when Mr. and Mrs. Graypeck are there."

"All right," groaned Joel. Then he asked Mom how long he was going to have to stay at the table.

"Just do your best," sighed Mom. All three of them were quiet the rest of the way home. Mom looked like she had a lot on her mind.

When they pulled into the garage Joel jumped out of the car the minute it stopped, and ran to the door.

"Joel," Mom called after him, "I could use a hand with some packages."

"Mom," Joel yelled back, "if I don't get to the bathroom, I'm going to have an accident."

"Jillian," said Mom, "please give me a hand with these groceries."

"That's so unfair Mom!" said Jelly Bean, standing with her arms folded. "Why do I have to help when Joel doesn't have to?"

After a minute or two she walked over to where Mom was bent over the trunk and helped her bring up all the bags from the supermarket. She really didn't like disappointing Mom.

Just as she was thinking what a pain Joel was, Roger-Over overheard Jelly Bean's footsteps coming up from the garage to the kitchen, ran up to her, licked her elbow and then her hands. After that he jumped up and tried to lick her face, but Mom yelled at him to get down. "Hey guy, I missed you!" Jelly Bean told him, leaning over and rubbing his fur till it looked all messy, "Let's go upstairs."

"Not now, Jillian," said Mom. "I need you to please round up your brothers for me. I need everyone's help right now."

"Michael! Sam! Joel!" Jelly Bean called, and then climbed up the stairs two by two and knocked on each of her brothers' doors. Roger-Over scampered along close behind her, wagging his tail. He liked this game. It didn't take much to make a dog happy.

After knocking on Michael's door, Jelly Bean spun back around to stare when he came out followed by a girl. She was the same girl who had been hanging around with him a lot lately. And as usual, she was wearing the most ripped-up jeans Jelly Bean had ever seen, with the loose, raggedy-looking tee-shirt she always had on. It must have been her favorite outfit – unless it was her only one – because it was the only outfit Jelly Bean ever saw her wearing. Her long dirty-looking brown hair hung all the way down her back, and covered one eye completely. Tattoos were all over both of her arms like big giant ugly decorations: one looked like a snake, and the other one looked like a scary witch face. Michael's visitor wasn't too friendly, either. Whenever she came out of his room, she practically flew down the stairs and out the door. When she passed so close to Jelly Bean that she couldn't avoid looking at her, she gave her just the teeniest smile. This time though when she went flying out the door, Roger-Over barked at her like crazy. She ran away faster than ever, like she was scared to death. Or she might have been embarrassed about hiding out in Michael's room.

In the kitchen Mom was giving everyone a job to do. "Jillian, you feed Roger-Over. I don't think he's been fed yet." Jelly Bean reached up to grab one of the cans of dog food from one of the cabinet shelves, and mixed it together with some of his dry food. Even though Roger-Over kept jumping up to try to reach his food bowl, Jelly Bean kept stirring the gross brown lumpy mixture around and around. She liked to get it exactly like Dad had shown her when they first brought Roger-Over home.

"Do you like that girl who's always in Michael's room?" Jelly Bean whispered to Mom, after she finally put Roger-Over's food down, and he was lapping it up like it might be his last meal ever.

"I don't know her well enough to comment," Mom answered softly. "I've never really talked to her, and she doesn't pause long enough to say hello or good-bye. From what I have seen of her, she doesn't seem to have any manners. Or maybe she's just shy," Mom added. She was looking down at the carrots she was peeling into thin slices, curling them, and placing them around her platter of grilled vegetables. Mom made the food she served look like it could be on a table in a fancy restaurant. She didn't always do it that way, but she could. Mom said she learned how to do it all from Grandma.

"How come she's always hiding out in Michael's room?" Jelly Bean asked Mom.

Joel burst out laughing. "Clueless," he said, shaking his head.

"You're done," Mom said to him, grabbing the silverware from him as he was about to finish putting it on the table.

"Dumb!" he called to Jelly Bean as he headed for the stairs. Mom gave him an angry look that he probably didn't even see. Then she yelled to him she was going to have to discuss his behavior with Dad. Joel scrambled back downstairs and begged Mom not to. That made Jelly Bean happy.

Mom sighed and pushed her hair off her forehead. "Don't let that dog get at the food," she told Jelly Bean, putting the platters in the middle of the table, as far away from Roger-Over as possible. Everything smelled so good, and Roger-Over must have thought so too.

"Can I go now?" Michael asked. "I'm done slicing up the bread." He stood next to Mom, with his hands in his pockets. Michael was about a head taller than she was now. Maybe even a little more than that.

"You're a mess!" Mom looked up at him, then shook her head and smiled. She reached up to push the hair out of his face.

"Ma!" He stepped back, and Mom couldn't reach him, which was kind of funny. His hair fell right back into his eyes.

"At least go get washed up," Mom told him.

"How come that girl's always in your room?" Jelly Bean asked him. Michael made an angry face, like he always did when Jelly Bean asked him anything. Mom said that was because people over a certain age didn't like answering personal questions.

"Guess she must like it in there," Michael explained, but not like he was serious. He rolled his eyes.

"Get ready for dinner!" Mom called after him, but Michael was already halfway up the stairs, climbing them three at a time. Jelly Bean wondered when his legs had gotten so long. Soon the music from his room was blaring. Michael's music was awful. He didn't use his earphones, but no one knew why. Mom said he was going through a stage.

The doorbell rang. Roger-Over barked at the top of his lungs, and Mom yelled to Jelly Bean she had to put him out in the back, because he was giving her a headache. Grandpa came in carrying about five grocery bags smushed together, each one filled to the top with cookies and fruit, a giant loaf of bread poking out of the top, and lots of other yummy things. Grandma came towards Jelly Bean with her arms open wide, and gave her a huge hug.

Then it was Grandpa's turn. He put down all the bags he was holding on the kitchen counter, turned around, and scooped her up. He gave Jelly Bean a big kiss and hug and asked how school was. "Not good at all," said Jelly Bean, playing with the gold buttons on Grandpa's vest. They walked into the den with their arms around each other. Sometimes it was fun being the youngest kid in the family, and the only girl. Nobody else got as much attention from Grandma and Grandpa, even though that was probably because they were all too busy. Grandpa told Jelly Bean that later he wanted to know all about what was going on in school, and what was bothering her exactly. But that was going to have to wait till later.

"Hi Sandy!" Grandma and Grandpa said to Mom, almost at the same time. They took turns kissing her.

Then Grandpa showed Mom what was in each of the four grocery bags he had brought. He took out all kinds of special salads and cakes, and everything smelled like pickles and cheese and onions and cinnamon and vanilla, all mixed together.

"I made my special yeast cake," said Grandma.

"Mmmmmmm," said Mom, unwrapping one of the packages on top that smelled so delicious. "Still warm," she said. "You're the best," she told Grandma. Grandma truly was the best baker in the whole world. Mom gave her a kiss on her cheek, and that made Grandma smile. Grandma and Grandpa helped Mom unpack the rest of the goodies.

"What a feast!" said Jelly Bean, taking Grandpa's hand, and leading him into the den, where they both plopped down on the couch. Jelly Bean picked up the remote that was squished in between the couch cushions, and clicked on the TV. She moved close to Grandpa, and he put his arm around her. She played with his stubby fingers that ended in big fat fingernails.

"Any good stories today?" she asked. Grandpa was great at telling stories about all the people he met while he traveled around for work. He was a salesman. Mom said people liked Grandpa so much because he always remembered things about them, and they could tell he really cared about them. Grandpa made everyone feel like they were each his good friend.

"No good stories today, Jilly."

"Aw, you sure?"

"I'm sure. And anyway, I want to know what's going on with you."

"Everyone in school hates me Grandpa," said Jelly Bean, looking down.

"That's not possible," he told her.

"Well, it's true," Jelly Bean said, in her saddest voice. She concentrated on pulling out one of the long gray hairs on one of his fingers.

"What are you trying to do to me?" Grandpa asked her. He made a funny noise as if she had hurt him, and rubbed his hand.

"You're getting fat!" Jelly Bean told him, patting his stomach.

"That's just my vest!" said Grandpa, trying to pull on his vest so it covered his whole stomach. That wasn't so easy to do. He laughed his funny laugh.

"You said that last time," Jelly Bean told him. She leaned back against Grandpa's chest. "I don't even feel like talking about school anymore," she said, folding her arms. "It's just icky. Even my teacher hates me." Grandpa tousled her hair and kissed her on the top of her head. They both watched the news for a while. An earthquake had just happened somewhere, a fire someplace else, and some of the bad guys police had caught were scary-looking. They made Jelly Bean think about what Britney had said about her dad. The reporters sounded angry. Then a sports reporter talked about some football games and players who had gotten hurt, and last of all the weatherman came on and said it was going to get colder.

Down came Sam and Joel, just when she had decided to ask Grandpa for some advice. They came up to Grandpa with a deck of cards, and asked him to show them some new tricks. Grandpa was amazing at card tricks, and Sam and Joel were always trying to learn new ones from him. "How'd you do that?" was all they ever said, after they couldn't figure out how to copy what Grandpa was doing. Grandpa told them all they had to do was pay closer attention.

"Come on, boy," Jelly Bean said to Roger-Over, giving up her place on the couch to head upstairs. "I'm getting squished here."

"Jillian, can you please come here?" Mom called from the kitchen. Intercepted again. Roger-Over scampered along after her, about an inch behind her heels.

"Mom I need to get washed up for dinner," Jelly Bean answered. It was a lie – sort of – but she knew Mom would leave her alone with that excuse. And, when she peeked into the kitchen on her way up, it looked like Mom was already getting a lot of help from Grandma.

What Jelly Bean needed was a few minutes of peace and quiet. When she got to her room, she shut the door and flopped down on her bed. "Gymnastics was great, Roge," she told him, as he curled up on the floor next to her. "I'm really good at it. Mrs. Clare told everyone to watch me, which was cool, especially since things at school have been pretty terrible. I hate school so much. Then, in the locker room, I started talking to Britney Keller." She flipped over. "She was really the one who started talking to me. We had never talked before. Ever. Now at least one other person in the class likes me, I mean aside from Heather Farrell. Heather's coming over tomorrow, and she wants to play with dolls. That's so babyish. I gave away all my dolls about a gazillion years ago. But, since no one else wanted to be my friend, it looks like I'm stuck with Heather. At least for tomorrow."

Jelly Bean reached down and carefully inspected the insides of Roger-Over's velvety ears, even though he wasn't being exactly patient while she poked around there. Then she flipped over on her back, and studied her ceiling for a few minutes while she felt sorry for herself. "On top of everything else, I really don't feel like meeting Suzanne's parents, Roge." He licked her hand, which was hanging off the side of her bed. Jelly Bean groaned. She got up and walked to her dresser. "I think," she told him, as she rummaged through each drawer and pulled out the oldest tee-shirt she could find, followed by a pair of worn-out sweatpants that had a lot of holes in them, "I'm going to give everyone a little surprise when I come down for dinner tonight. I'm going to shake things up a little, as Ms. Peiser would say." After Jelly Bean changed, she put her hair into two of the messiest pigtails she could make, one high and one low.

No one said anything to Jelly Bean during dinner. But Grandma and Grandpa looked like they were bursting to say something, and Mom shot her some pretty angry looks.

Joel looked like he was going to say something mean, but instead he spit out his food when she came downstairs and sat there laughing to himself and shaking his head. Everyone was mostly interested in talking to Suzanne and her parents, who both looked even stranger than Jelly Bean had made herself look.

During dinner, mean old Suzanne kept looking over at her and giving Uncle Jack disgusted looks. She didn't have a great view of him from her seat on the other side way down at the other end of the table, but she was almost sure he raised his eyebrows in the funny way he sometimes did, and then smiled at Suzanne. She just kept looking back at him like she smelled something bad.

Mrs. Graypeck, Suzanne's mom, was tall and huge, and Mr. Graypeck was short, skinny, and completely bald. Mrs. Graypeck's hair was piled up in a huge bun on top of her head, with a shiny silver pin stuck in the front of it. She had on big shiny earrings that hung down almost to her shoulders. Her dress was bright pink and very tight. It looked like it was a costume. Mr. and Mrs. Graypeck both worked in the bakery they owned, and Mom and Grandma were asking them a lot of questions about what desserts they made there and how they made them. The Graypecks both talked with accents, so that it was hard to understand a single word they were saying. Mrs. Graypeck's voice kept getting really high, like a screeching bird. A lot of what she talked about had to do with dough and how long different desserts had to be in the oven. Mr. Graypeck talked a lot while she was talking, mostly to Dad, about their taxes and different kinds of people he didn't like who were moving into their neighborhood. He said "okay" a lot, making it sound like he was asking a question, and he pounded his fist on the table a few times, which made everyone look surprised. The first time he did that it made Jelly Bean jump. Dad looked like he was trying hard to act interested. It was impossible not to stare at them.

After dinner, Mr. Graypeck sat in the den with Dad and Grandpa. Jelly Bean walked through the den to see what they were doing, and she found Dad on the couch looking bored. The leg he had crossed over the other one was bouncing up and down, and he was turned slightly to the side. Obviously, Dad was trying to hide that he was checking messages on his phone. Jelly Bean sat on the edge of Dad's chair for a few minutes. Mr. Graypeck kept talking away in a loud fast way, something about politics. It sounded like he was worried the government was threatening to take away all his money. He said this president was a socialist. Now he was talking much louder than he needed to, especially since the people he was talking to were practically right next to him. He was leaning forward in his chair, and sounded all worked up. Dad nodded from time to time, and so did Grandpa. Grandpa sneaked a look at his watch a few times. She wondered if Dad would stay awake. It looked like he might not.

Jelly Bean had enough, so she walked into the kitchen, where Mom and Grandma were talking to Suzanne and Mrs. Graypeck. Roger-Over followed her in, but Suzanne turned away quickly and whispered something to her mother. "Can you please get the dog away from here," Mrs. Graypeck said to Jelly Bean. Roger-Over didn't look like he liked the two of them very much either, and he growled at Mrs. Graypeck. She jumped and gave a little scream, and said in her accent that she was not an animal lover. Jelly Bean was almost hoping Roger-Over would bite her so they would all have to leave. But she also knew if that happened it probably wouldn't turn out too well. Suzanne kept scrunching her eyes down to slits, and looking at Jelly Bean like she made her sick.

"Come on, Roge," said Jelly Bean, leading him upstairs to look for Uncle Jack, who was just coming out of the bathroom. "Where have you been?" she asked him.   It smelled like he had just poured a whole bottle of men's perfume all over himself.

"Hey," said Uncle Jack, squatting down to face Jelly Bean, "why the long face? And the crazy get-up?"

"All these new things keep happening," Jelly Bean blurted out. "I liked everything better the old way. I can't get used to everything new!" She wasn't sure how it happened, but she found herself crying into Uncle Jack's shirt. He slung his arm around her, and let her finish crying. She leaned against him and they went into her room. She sat on the edge of her bed, and he crouched in front of her. She put her arms on both his shoulders, and then they both started laughing, because he clunked to the floor in a funny way.

"Things change, Jilly," he told her when he got up. "People get married, and new people come into your life. They have children, they get different jobs, they move – all kinds of things like that. Nothing much ever really stays the same. Not for too long, anyway."

"Are you still going to come over?" she asked him. "I mean, without Suzanne? Sometimes?"

"Aw, come on, Jel," Uncle Jack said. She turned away from him to face the wall. Nothing ever worked out the way she wanted it to, Jelly Bean concluded, fighting back tears.

"It's not fair," she told him. She knew she was acting like a big baby, but she didn't care.

"Hey!" said Suzanne, all of a sudden barging in. "Is this private, or can I come in too?"

Ugh, thought Jelly Bean, *why do you have to be here?* She narrowed her eyes into slits, and grabbing onto her pillow, curled herself into a ball. All of a sudden, she felt nauseous.

"Of course, you can come in," Uncle Jack said to Suzanne, grabbing her and giving her a big hug and kiss.

Jelly Bean hated Suzanne for taking Uncle Jack away from her.

"She okay?" she heard Suzanne whisper to Uncle Jack. She sounded impatient. They stood in the doorway, very close together. Uncle Jack had his arms around her. Jelly Bean looked up at both of them with her saddest expression, but they looked like they had forgotten she was even alive.

"She'll be fine," Jelly Bean heard him answer. They walked a few steps away from her door, but Jelly Bean could still see them in the hallway. They were busy kissing, and that lasted a long time.

"Come back down," Suzanne yelled back to her, when they finally broke apart. But it didn't sound like she really meant it. So this is what things were going to be like from now on with Uncle Jack.

"Send in Roge," Jelly Bean called after them.

"Okie-doke," Uncle Jack called back. He sounded far away.

Then the room was spinning around and around. Roger-Over pushed the door open with his nose in his cute way, and padded in to lie next to her bed. Jelly Bean groaned.

"I feel really sick, Roge," Jelly Bean told him. "I hope I don't throw up on you. I ate so many of those cookies. Uncle Jack's never going to have time for me anymore, I can tell. Everyone was giving me funny looks because of my stupid outfit, and now Mom's probably mad. I'll just lie here for a little while, and maybe I'll feel better. Or maybe I'll just stay in my room forever." Roger-Over licked her hand, which was hanging off her bed again. "Wonder if anyone would notice if I just disappeared." Roger-Over understood. He always did. Dogs were so much more understanding than humans. She shut her eyes so the room would stay still.

Jelly Bean woke up sometime later, to feel Mom touching her arm. "You did it again Jilly. You fell asleep in your clothes. Come on," she said, sitting on the edge of Jelly Bean's bed, smoothing her forehead, "I'll help you change into your pj's."

"No!" Jelly Bean groaned. "Don't make me get up. I have a stomachache."

"I did see you taking a lot of those cookies Suzanne's parents brought," said Mom. "They were very rich. I don't usually keep that kind of dessert in the house," said Mom. She helped Jelly Bean get to the bathroom, and then out of her crazy outfit and into her pajamas.

"Don't mention those cookies to me anymore – ever!" said Jelly Bean, leaning over and holding her stomach on the way back to her room. As soon as they got back there, she flopped down on her bed.

"You'll feel better in the morning," said Mom.

"I doubt it," said Jelly Bean, groaning.

"Do you want a glass of ginger ale?" Mom asked.

"Yes," said Jelly Bean. "I mean no. Don't go." She pulled Mom back by her blouse, but then let go, and fell back on her bed. Roger-Over leaped up to lick her. "Down boy," said Jelly Bean.

"I have to go down, Jilly," said Mom. "And I have to let him out too. I don't think he's been out in a while. Dad fell right to sleep, as soon as everybody left." Mom yawned. "Besides, I'm about to fall off my feet."

"They were weird!" said Jelly Bean, and turned over on her side. "Didn't you think so?" she called to Mom after she went out into the hall.

"Oh, I guess they're a little different than we are," said Mom, coming back to Jelly Bean's door. She leaned against it, looking like her eyes were about to shut. Jelly Bean wondered if Mom agreed with her about Suzanne's parents but just didn't want to say so. Adults were funny that way. They always acted like they were afraid to admit things – even when they were obvious. "But you have to try to be tolerant of all different kinds of people," Mom was saying. This is the person that Uncle Jack wants to marry, and these people are her parents. They're not so terrible, really." It looked like Mom was trying not to smile, and she had a funny look on her face. "Okay, maybe they're a little bit – unusual," said Mom.

"Will I have to see them ever again?" Jelly Bean asked, turning back on her stomach. "Ooh, I don't feel so good."

"No, probably just every now and again." Mom yawned.

"All right, try to get some rest. And not so many cookies next time, especially not when they're the fancy kind with all that chocolate cream in the middle."

"Mom!" Jelly Bean called after her when she started walking away.

"What, Jillian?" Now Mom sounded annoyed.

"How come I don't get any attention anymore?"

Dad came to her doorway, and put his arm around Mom. She leaned her head on his shoulder. He was a lot taller than Mom was. Especially now that she had taken off her shoes.

"So is that what that silly outfit was about tonight? Getting some attention?" Mom was shaking her head. "Oh, Jillian."

Jelly Bean tried hard not to laugh, but finally she couldn't help it. "You guys didn't even notice!" She looked down. "Nobody did."

"We didn't want to make a scene at the table, Jilly. But you must have felt a little ridiculous," said Mom.

"Do I have to admit it?" Jelly Bean asked. They all laughed.

"Whatever happened to your part in the play?" asked Dad, as he and Mom were just about out the door. She had to cover her eyes, because the light from the hall was shining into them.

"Oh that," said Jelly Bean, groaning. "You don't need to bother even coming to it. I have the stupidest part ever." She told them all about what her part was going to be.

"Oh dear," said Mom.

"It's okay, you can laugh," Jelly Bean told her. "I'll take some more ginger ale now," she said to Mom.

"Well," said Dad, as Mom went downstairs, "it sounds like Ms. Peiser was just trying to do her best to include everyone."

"Dad," said Jelly Bean, "come on." She was too tired to explain anything else. And once adults had made up their mind about something, they didn't let in too many new ideas.

"It's been a long day for everyone," said Mom, coming back with her refilled glass of ginger ale.

"Thanks Mom," said Jelly Bean. She gave Mom a little hug, took a sip and lay back.

The thoughts of her awful part in the play, her "stardom" in gymnastics and her new friendship with Britney, and all the weird things that happened at dinner with those strange new people all swirled together and spun and tumbled inside her brain, as Jelly Bean worked on finding a comfortable position and then felt herself drifting off to sleep.

Chapter 6

In Which Roger-Over Gets Away and Gets Rescued

The next day, just as Jelly Bean had been afraid of, Heather came over with not one, not two, but three of her dolls. "Oh great," Jelly Bean said to Roger-Over, as she kneeled on her bed and watched out her window as Heather got out of her car. One doll was gigantic, nearly as big as Heather was, so her mother had to help her get to the door with it. The others were normal doll-size, but one was dressed in something that looked like an old-fashioned fancy outfit, with gloves and a veil. The last one had long hair and a perfect figure like the old Barbie dolls that Mom had told her were popular when she was growing up. It was going to be a long day.

"Your sister still plays with dolls?" Jelly Bean heard Michael's girlfriend say to him, as she passed them on her way down the stairs to the den. They were lying together on Michael's bed watching tv, but then they got up and came down to sit on the couch, where they took up a lot of space. They stuck their bare feet up on the coffee table, and none of their feet looked too clean. Mom would have a fit if she came in, thought Jelly Bean. Too bad she had to pass right in front of them on her way to the front door, but there they were.

"I don't know, I guess so," Michael was saying. He had trouble staying still. "Who cares if she plays with dolls? I couldn't care less. I'm going to get some food," he told her.

"Are you ever not hungry?" his girlfriend asked. She had to be his girlfriend, Jelly Bean decided.   It looked like she was wearing the same jeans she always wore, and a sweatshirt that said in big letters "Give a damn."

"What's your name?" Jelly Bean finally got up the courage to ask, as she waited by the door for Heather to say good-bye to her mom and haul in her last doll.

"Cameron," she answered. Then she stared at Jelly Bean for a long time, before she got up to follow Michael into the kitchen. She reached up to put her hands on his shoulders, and she had to stand on tiptoe to do that. The two of them always acted so weird together.

Jelly Bean opened the door for Heather.

"Hi, Jelly Bean!" Heather said. "Look who wanted to come with me. I didn't think you'd mind." Cameron obviously heard this, because she practically collapsed laughing on Michael's back while he was hunting around in each of the cabinets for snacks.

"Come on upstairs Heather," Jelly Bean said. She was anxious to get away from Michael and Cameron.

"Leave her alone," Michael said to Cameron, pushing her away. She pushed him back and then they kept pushing each other. Cameron's long hair was flying all over the place. It looked more like they were playing a game than trying to hurt each other. Sort of. Jelly Bean stood still on the stairs where she could watch.

"Ow," Cameron told him, finally. "That really hurt." She rubbed her hip. "Your sister's still watching us, you know," Cameron told him. And it was true, Jelly Bean couldn't stop staring at them from the top of the stairs.

"Come on, Jelly Bean," Heather said to her. "I came here to play with you, not watch your brother and his girlfriend all day."

But even after Jelly Bean shut her door, she kept hearing them laughing. Finally she got up from her bed where she had flopped down, ran downstairs and started punching him with all her strength. She didn't get very far though, and before she knew it, he grabbed her wrists. Jelly Bean kept her elbows at her sides as Michael lifted her high up and threw her on the couch in the den. Out of the corner of her eye, Jelly Bean saw Heather watching their fight from the stop of the stairs, while she chewed on her fingers. Heather's eyes were open wide.

"Mike, you better be careful," said Cameron, watching Jelly Bean kick like crazy. "You're going to hurt her." But Jelly Bean couldn't reach Michael, who jumped up and ran into the kitchen where he ducked down, so she couldn't see where he went.

"Boo!" he said, jumping out from behind the table. Jelly Bean jumped and started laughing.

"She's tough," he said to Cameron. She leaned against the side of the entrance to the kitchen. He stuck his face right close up to hers and made some dumb noises. Cameron cracked up, and he made some funny faces at her. The two of them must have completely forgotten about Heather, the dolls, and her.

Then as if the two of them weren't acting crazy enough, Cameron leaned forward and bit Michael on his nose. Holding his nose, he gave a loud yelp and let go of her, just as Mom and Dad came back from their walk. Cameron just missed backing up smack into Dad, who quickly moved to the side. When Mom and Dad asked Michael what was going on, Cameron fled out the door and leaned against Michael's car. Jelly Bean couldn't stop watching Cameron. You never knew what the two of them were going to do next.

"Nothin'," he told them, holding his nose where it must have still hurt, then plopped down on the couch and turned the TV on loud. From where Jelly Bean stood, she heard Sam and Joel both come out of their rooms almost at the same time, and race each other to the bathroom. Sam must have gotten there first, because Joel started banging on the door, whining and screaming at him.

"Go use the other bathroom!" Sam yelled at him from inside. Joel gave the door one last pound, and then ran to the bathroom in Mom and Dad's room. He almost tripped and fell on the way over a shoe someone had left in the hallway. Those two didn't usually fight too much, but when they did it was pretty crazy.

"Your house is wild Jelly Bean," said Heather, who looked happy to be back in Jelly Bean's room, with the door shut behind them.

"Hold on," said Jelly Bean. "I need to see where my dog is."

"But Jelly Bean, can I just introduce you to my dolls first?" Heather called after her. "They really want to meet you!" Sure enough, Heather had lined up all her dolls against Jelly Bean's wall, next to her desk. Jelly Bean stood with her arms folded, wanting to head downstairs so badly. At first, she tried not to look annoyed, but then she gave up even trying to do that.

"I'd like you to meet Polly, Molly, and Holly," said Heather.

"Wowie," said Jelly Bean, feeling like she might explode. "Wowie, Heather."

"I know you're going to get to like them as much as I do Jelly Bean, once you get to know them," said Heather, sounding so enthusiastic. And too clueless to notice how unhappy Jelly Bean looked. Or maybe she just didn't care. "Now watch. I'm going to give them their mid-morning snack."

Jelly Bean groaned, plopped down on her bed and held her head between her hands. Then right when Heather was in the middle of feeding Polly, Molly, and Holly their pretend food, Sam opened the door and stuck his head in. "Oh sorry," he said, looking surprised, "I didn't know you were busy."

"Sam! Wait!" Jelly Bean called loudly. She ran to the door and opened it. "What were you going to say?" Turning to Heather, she quickly told her, "You give your dolls their snack. I'll be right back." Running out the door, Jelly Bean almost fell over Roger-Over. "Sorry guy," she said to him, and he followed her down the stairs. "Sam, come back!" she yelled again. But he had gone into his room and shut the door.

Just then the doorbell rang. Jelly Bean watched from the bottom of the stairs as Mom went to answer the door. She was about to sign for a package, when Roger-Over took off like a shot out the open door, because he must have seen a bird or a squirrel, or maybe a rabbit. In a split second he was out of sight. Jelly Bean couldn't believe her eyes. She had never seen him act that disobedient before, but he had probably gotten overexcited from all the commotion that had been going on in the house.

"Dad! Michael! Sam! Joel! Help!" Jelly Bean screamed. Mom rushed away from the door and called everyone in her loudest voice too. Sam was the first to come bounding down the stairs and as soon as Mom and Jelly Bean explained what had just happened, he ran into the yard and then to each neighbor's house on the street, one by one, to look in each one's front and back yards.

Michael came down and when they told him what had happened, he ran around the house to the backyard and began checking each house on the street behind them. "I'll go over to the creek," he called to them, "and to the new houses they're building." Joel came down and said he'd go over two streets to look behind those houses. Mom told him to be careful because sometimes there was a lot of traffic on Hartley Road and Butler Parkway.

"You check the houses on our street!" Sam yelled to Jelly Bean. Mom said she had to wait till Dad came down to go with her.

Jelly Bean bounced up and down and hung on to Mom's hand. "My doggie, my doggie," she kept saying.

"I'll wait here with your friend," Mom told Jelly Bean. Heather had come down to the bottom of the stairs with one of her dolls. She looked very unhappy.

"I have to go find my dog, Heather," Jelly Bean told her. Then for a long time she and Dad ran from one house to the next, calling Roger-Over's name, but they finally had to give up looking for him, because Dad was out of breath and Jelly Bean was so tired and sweaty, she could hardly move anymore. She felt like she was going to collapse right on one of the neighbors' lawns. Some of the older neighbors were looking at her from their windows. Mrs. Mahoney was shaking her head. Mrs. Miller came outside, but Jelly Bean just said "no thanks" when she asked if she could help. What could poor old Mrs. Miller do anyway, she was so bent over and moved so slowly. Mr. Maguire came outside, and offered to call some people.

When Dad got his breath back, he said thanks to all the people who had come out to offer help. As they walked back home, Dad put his arm around Jelly Bean, and wiped his forehead with his other hand.

Covering her eyes with her hands, Jelly Bean banged open the front door with her foot. She ran into the kitchen and flopped down on the chair next to Mom. She leaned forward, put her head on her arms, and wailed.

"I was just on the phone with the police," said Mom, looking away from her laptop. "I know they'll find him." She pushed Jelly Bean's hair back from her head, where it was all sticky with sweat. Mom tried to hug her, but Jelly Bean kept her head down and cried till her shoulders shook.

"You don't know that Mom," she said between sobs. Jelly Bean slumped down in her chair and covered her eyes, feeling sadder than she'd ever felt in her life. "You know they don't always find people's dogs. And he can run as fast as a deer when he's chasing something." She knew Mom was remembering the same thing she was, when Roger-Over chased a rabbit last spring, but luckily came back home after the rabbit finally outran him.

Mom looked at Jelly Bean over her half-glasses. "I know one of the boys will find him Jilly. He can't have gone too far." She knew that Mom was trying to sound like she meant it. "Go be with your friend now Jillian. She's been by herself a long time. Please trust me that we'll find Roge."

"All right," said Jelly Bean, even though she didn't feel like doing what Mom had asked at all. Her eyes hurt from crying and she couldn't stop sobbing. She walked slowly, and just as she reached the stairs, she ran into Heather on her way down.

"I was very hurt, Jelly Bean," Heather told her. "You left me alone for a long time. And my dollies were hurt too." Heather gave Jelly Bean an angry look. "I just put them down for their nap."

"Heather, my dog ran away," Jelly Bean told her, "and we can't find him anywhere." She stared at her and thought about what a bad idea it had been to invite her over.

"Jelly Bean, there is so much noise in your house. I have to see if it woke up my dollies." Heather obviously couldn't care less about Roger-Over.

"But Heather, your dolls aren't even alive. I mean they're not even real."

"They are to me Jelly Bean," said Heather.

"Oh," said Jelly Bean. She didn't know what else to say. She was so worried it hurt.

"Heather dear," Mom asked, "is your house very quiet all the time?"

"Yes," answered Heather. "Especially when my dollies are sleeping," she explained.

When Heather went upstairs to check on her dolls, Jelly Bean went back into the kitchen. Mom said to her, "When you invite someone over, honey, you should try and make sure they have a good time." She could tell Mom was trying hard to say the right thing.

"I can't concentrate on anything else now, Ma. I just lost my best friend in the whole world." Jelly Bean threw herself against Mom's arm.

"Jillian," said Mom, "I know Roger-Over's going to come back. I just know it." She rubbed Jelly Bean's back.

"It's just too hard right now, Mom!" Jelly Bean told her, and started wailing all over again. Mom handed her some tissues, and she blew her nose into them. She knew she looked like a sweaty mess, but she didn't care at all.

Soon Sam walked in, banging the door shut behind him, and sat down in a kitchen chair across from Jelly Bean. "No luck," he said, wiping his hand across his forehead. It was dripping wet. "I don't know where that dog went." He got up to get a water bottle from the refrigerator. "I looked all over."

Dad came back in looking exhausted. He had gone out again after Jelly Bean came back home. "Couldn't find him anywhere," he said. Mom told Dad he needed to go upstairs to lie down for a while. Two minutes later Dad came back down. "Jilly," he asked her, sounding kind of confused, holding a washcloth to his forehead, "did you put some dolls in our bed?"

"No Dad," said Jelly Bean, busy thinking about whether or not she'd ever see Roger-Over again. "I know who did though," she added miserably, heading upstairs to ask Heather if she wanted something for lunch.

Michael came into the kitchen with Cameron, who must have decided to come back. "Maybe those dolls can sub for Roger-Over while he's missing," he said to Jelly Bean.

"You shut up," she told him. "Mom, tell him to be quiet." She started crying really loudly now.

"Michael," Mom ordered, "leave your sister alone. I'll drive around a little, to see if I can spot Roger-Over anywhere."

"Thank you, Mom, thank you," said Jelly Bean, giving her a huge hug, and covering her with kisses. Mom grabbed her jacket and headed out to the car. "Please can I go with you?" Jelly Bean asked, even though she knew Mom's answer would be "no."

Mom came back after a little while and told Jelly Bean she hadn't had any luck either. She started suggesting things Jelly Bean could do with Heather to keep her mind off Roger-Over being missing. All Jelly Bean felt like doing was staring out her window and moping. Sam helped her make some signs with markers and oaktag he had in his closet about a missing dog, while Heather played some game with her dolls that Dad had brought back in. After lunch – which Jelly Bean tried to eat – Heather said she was going to call her mom because she wanted to go home, but her mom said she wasn't going to be able to pick her up until a little later.

After suggesting a few other ideas, Mom got Jelly Bean interested in making Halloween costumes with Heather, but only after Mom promised she'd call the police again and try making some other calls too. Then Mom took a big bag of old clothes she was going to give to homeless people, and Jelly Bean and Heather both thought up some ideas for costumes. Mom also gave them some large pieces of material she had shown some of her customers that they had decided they didn't want.

Mom ended up helping Heather make a ballerina outfit, which looked kind of silly, but Heather seemed to like it. She helped Jelly Bean make a sailor suit out of an outfit Sam had worn when he was younger. Mom helped her change the pants into shorts, cut the sleeves and add a tie around the neck using one that used to be Dad's. Jelly Bean knew Mom was trying hard to make her forget about Roger-Over, which worked for a little while. She couldn't stop thinking about him, and wondering whether he'd come back, no matter how much Mom talked about how great their costumes were turning out. Grandma always said Mom could have been a wonderful artist.

"Wow!" said Mom, when the girls were done. Then she had to go downstairs because Grace Applebaum came over. She was one of the people Mom was helping decide how to decorate her new home. Jelly Bean's room was closest to the top of the stairs, so she could hear everything that went on downstairs. Mom sounded like she was trying to stay patient with Grace, even though she kept asking over and over "but what if this?" and "what if that?"

"Come here, sweetheart," Grace said to Jelly Bean when she saw her at the top of the stairs. "I remember when my Sarah was your age. And now she's a big grown-up married lady!" Jelly Bean made a face. Every time Mrs. Applebaum saw her, all she ever talked about was Sarah. A long time ago, Sarah used to baby-sit for Jelly Bean and her brothers. But one night when she was there, they all had a big pillow fight that turned into a huge mess all over the house, and after that Sarah never wanted to come back. Jelly Bean couldn't really blame her.

Grace Applebaum was still talking, pretty much non-stop.

"I know," Jelly Bean finished the sentence Grace was in the middle of, "she's studying to be a nutritionist."

Grace Applebaum clapped her hands together and laughed. "You remembered! Sandy, this one's brilliant," she told Mom. Jelly Bean wondered what in the world was so brilliant about remembering the same thing someone said every single time she came over.

Finally, Heather's mother came to pick her up. Heather left, loaded down with the Halloween costume she had made, and all her dolls. She dragged two of them behind her down the walk. Thank goodness, Jelly Bean thought to herself, even though making the costumes had been fun. Sort of.

Jelly Bean hung around the kitchen, pacing back and forth until Grace Applebaum finally left. She felt like she was going to burst. "Mom," she called, as soon as she heard Mom and Grace say good-bye to each other, and the door shut, "I need to go out and look for Roger-Over again. I really, really need to! I'm so worried about him Mom, I'm going crazy."

Mom gave Jelly Bean a giant hug. "I know how you feel, Jillian. I'm worried about him too. All right, see if you can get one of your brothers to go help you look again before it to gets dark. I need go up and lie down for a little while, before I have to get ready to go out."

Jelly Bean got Sam to go look for Roger-Over with her, and they looked all over the neighborhood again. But no Roger-Over anywhere. "Sam," said Jelly Bean, on the long walk home, "where is he?"

"I don't know, Jilly. Maybe a policeman will find him, if we're lucky. Or maybe someone already found him roaming around, and took him home with them. You know, so he wouldn't get run over." Sam didn't sound like he completely believed what he said. He sounded more worried than she had ever heard him sound.

"You mean now all we can do is wait? What about flyers? Would you help me make some more Sam? We could put them in people's mailboxes." Jelly Bean looked at him, but he didn't want to look back at her. "I know Mom put a lot of stuff online about Roge." Jelly Bean almost choked on his name when she said it. Sam kept looking down at the ground.

"Okay," said Sam, as they trudged home, "I can help you do that." Sam threw his arm around Jelly Bean's shoulders.

As soon as they got home Jelly Bean was all set to work on the flyers with Sam, when the most wonderful surprise was waiting for them. Aidan Brown, a boy from the neighborhood who was the littlest kid in her grade and whose hair and clothes always looked a mess, was sitting in the den with Roger-Over.

"Aidan?" said Jelly Bean, rushing over to Roger-Over. She wasn't quite sure what he was doing there, or how come Roger-Over didn't run over to her when he saw her. Or why he barely even raised up his head. Thank goodness the best pet in the whole wide world was back, but something wasn't right.

"Aidan's been telling us, honey, how he saved Roger-Over," said Mom, sitting in her bathrobe. Her make-up was halfway on, which made her look a little silly. But nothing else really mattered at all, as long as Roger-Over was back.

"What happened to him?" cried Jelly Bean, putting her head down on him as he lay on the carpet, not barking at all, just whimpering, and barely moving a muscle. He was all wet and covered with dirt. "Bad dog!" she said to him – but lovingly, so he could tell how glad she was to see him, "Why did you run away like that? You could have gotten yourself killed!"

"So I wrapped him up in my jacket," Aidan was saying, "just like we learned to do in cub scouts."

"They really taught you how to do that?" Jelly Bean asked. None of her brothers had ever had any interest in cub scouts. At least she never remembered hearing it talked about.

"But Aidan," Mom asked, "how did you get him back here, from all the way over by the highway?"

"My parents and I were driving back from my aunt's house," Aidan explained. "I thought I saw your dog lying by the side of the road, so I called out to them to stop. My dad pulled over, we both got out, and he helped me load him into the backseat of the car, so he could ride on my lap. He was a dead weight. We thought he either must have been hit there, or maybe someone dragged him over there. I mean to the side of the road."

"My dog was hit by a car?" Jelly Bean asked. She was picturing Roger-Over laying by the side of the road.

Mom nodded, reaching over to stroke Jelly Bean's back. "It's a good thing Aidan found him and brought him back to you," said Mom gently.

"Oh my god! Oh my god!" Jelly Bean cried, jumping up and down. She couldn't help herself. "He could have been killed!"

"Jillian, what do you say to Aidan for rescuing Roger-Over?"

"Thank you, Aidan," said Jelly Bean, looking at Aidan like he was the biggest hero she had ever seen. She had never noticed him much in school, he was so quiet and shy. It seemed to Jelly Bean as if he barely ever spoke to anybody, and that the other kids barely spoke to him. Once he had come to school with his pants on backwards. But something Jelly Bean did know after the last few days of school was what it felt like to be made fun of and ignored, and she decided she was going to tell everyone what an amazing person Aidan was. Everyone who would talk to her, that is.

"You're a hero," Jelly Bean told him. Aidan turned bright red. Mom had given him a chocolate doughnut and milk when he first came in, so now the mustache he had from drinking the milk made his face around his mouth look all white. Jelly Bean smiled at him, and Aidan smiled back in a shy way. Then Aidan's dad came to the door, and after everyone thanked him and told him what an amazing son he had, he told Aidan he needed to leave because there was someplace they had to go.

"Good-bye boy," Aidan said to Roger-Over in a gentle way, and leaned down to pet him softly. He left the house with the biggest smile on his face. As he went to his car with his dad, he was walking straight and tall. He still did look way too small to be in her same grade, Jelly Bean thought to herself.

After Aidan left, Jelly Bean couldn't stop hugging and kissing Roger-Over, who just lay on Aidan's jacket, even though Mom told her not to do that because she could get germs. Roger-Over sounded like he was crying in a doggie way. He kept looking up at Jelly Bean with big sad eyes, and then shutting them. "Why on earth did you run away, you silly thing?" she turned her head to ask him, as he lay there looking like a furry bag of bones. Roger-Over feebly picked up one paw, and put it on her leg. "Good boy," she told him. "And never let me catch you running out the door without your leash on again. You could have gotten yourself killed!" She put her face right up to his, ignoring Mom who kept telling her to stop.

"He needs to get to the vet right away," said Sam.

"Hey guy," said Jelly Bean again, stroking his messy fur, "you could have died."

"You're such a drama queen," said Michael, who all of a sudden was standing over her. But when Jelly Bean looked up at him, he was brushing away a few tears.

Mom called Dr. Pfeiffer, Roger-Over's vet, who said he was just about to close up his office for the day, but that he'd wait for them to bring Roger-Over since it was an emergency. Mom and Dad had to get ready to go out, and they had to get to the city by a certain time, so Michael said he'd drive Roger-Over there. Dad carefully wrapped poor Roge in a blanket, and carried him out to the car with Michael helping. Jelly Bean and Sam got in the backseat first, and Dad and Michael laid Roger-Over on both their laps. He picked his head up for a minute, to lick Jelly Bean's face, and then fell back with a little whimper. Jelly Bean put her head down and snuggled into his fur.

Michael's friend Brady pulled up just then and got in the passenger seat. He looked a lot like Michael, only skinnier. They both had on the exact same kind of jeans, and the exact same jeans jacket.

"You guys look like twins," Jelly Bean told them. Brady told Jelly Bean he thought that was hilarious. He and Michael looked at each other and cracked up. At first Jelly Bean was proud of herself for making them laugh, but then realized they were laughing at her for saying something dumb. Oh well.

"Sorry about what happened to your dog," Brady turned around and said to them.

"He got run over by a car," Jelly Bean told him.

"So I heard," said Brady. He whistled, and then made his mouth stretch all the way to both sides of his face, which made him look worried. When they pulled up to the front of Dr. Pfeiffer's office, Michael dropped off Jelly Bean, Sam and Roger-Over, and said they'd be back to pick them up when they were done. The two of them always seemed to have someplace to go.

Jelly Bean and Sam carefully carried in Roger-Over, who was pretty heavy. No other people – or animals – were there, and Dr. Pfeiffer looked like he was packing up his things and getting ready to leave. He wasn't even wearing his doctor's coat anymore. He was just wearing jeans and a gray tee-shirt. When they came in with Roger-Over he smiled and took a quick look at his watch.

"It's a break, but fortunately it's not a bad break," Dr. Pfeiffer told them, as he sponged off Roger-Over and wrapped his back leg up in a big, stiff bandage, while the patient made little crying sounds.

"What should we do for him at home?" Sam asked.

"Treat him exactly as you would normally," Dr. Pfeiffer explained, "except don't play with him roughly. He won't be able to run around for a few weeks, and he's going to be hobbling for a while. He may not be as hungry as usual, but you don't need to be concerned. You do need to treat his leg with care, and bring him back in a week. Or by all means bring him back sooner if you notice anything that doesn't look quite right to you."

Dr. Pfeiffer finished drying off Roger-Over, while Jelly Bean tried to pay close attention to what Dr. Pfeiffer was telling them. When he was done wrapping up his leg, they thanked him. Then she texted Michael, and she and Sam and Roger-Over waited outside on Dr. Pfeiffer's front steps till he came back for them.

"I might want to study to be a veterinarian after college," Sam said to Jelly Bean.

"I thought college was where you learn how to do what you're going to do when you're grown up," said Jelly Bean. This was something she had been wondering about. Luckily Sam wasn't the type who made her feel dumb when she asked questions some people would think were stupid.

"Yes, often it is," he told her. "But not all the time. Sometimes people have to go on to graduate school."

"Oh," said Jelly Bean. "When do you have to decide?" she asked. She had been curious about that question too.

"For each person it's different," Sam told her. "The sooner you know, the better. I think so, anyway."

"But how do you decide? Does an idea just pop into your head one day?" Jelly Bean looked over at Sam. She stroked Roger-Over. This whole idea sounded complicated, but she knew she did have some time to figure it all out.

"Well," said Sam, "someone might suggest something to you that you might be good at, or something could happen that might make you become interested in a certain career. Like Roge here, breaking his leg." He patted the most wonderful dog in the world, who responded by looking up at Sam and whining softly.

"Careful," said Jelly Bean. "Don't hurt him."

"Is someone picking you two up soon?" asked Dr. Pfeiffer behind them, locking the door to his office, and walking down the little staircase. When he was at the bottom of the steps, he looked up at them.

"We're waiting for our brother to pick us up," Sam answered. "Jilly, maybe you should text him again," he said to her. "Find out if he's close." He chewed his lip for a minute. "Can I ask you something about becoming a vet, Dr. Pfeiffer?"

"Sure, Sam," said Dr. Pfeiffer, leaning against the railing right next to them, and taking a quick look at his phone. "How can I help you?" Dr. Pfeiffer asked, and then yawned a gigantic yawn. "Sorry," he said. "It's been a long day."

"What do you need to study in college to become a vet?" he asked. At first it didn't look like Dr. Pfeiffer was paying much attention to Sam, but he must have been. Even though he did look tired all right.

Dr. Pfeiffer stuck his phone back in his front pocket, and leaned down to stroke Roger-Over while he talked. "Well, you have to take quite a few science and math courses. Then, when you're done with college, you have to go to veterinarian school, which is a special kind of medical school. That's where you learn all about animals and how to care for them and help them when they're sick or have other medical problems. There aren't that many veterinarian schools in this country, so some people end up having to go study in a foreign country."

"I was thinking I might like to become a vet," said Sam. He looked up at Dr. Pfeiffer, then down again at Roger-Over. He folded his arms.

"It's hard work Sam," Dr. Pfeiffer answered. "Most days I enjoy what I do, same as most people, I suppose, if you asked them. If you still feel the same way when you get to college, I'd be glad to talk to you some more about it. It is a very rewarding career," he added. "And your patients can't argue with you about the treatment you recommend." He winked and chuckled. After a moment, Jelly Bean laughed too.

"Thanks, Dr. Pfeiffer," said Sam. Jelly Bean thanked him too.

"Good night now," he said, when Michael and Brady pulled up. It felt good to pile in their car with Roger-Over, before it gets too dark, and a lot colder too.

That night Michael and Sam were both going out, so Jelly Bean had to stay home with Joel and Pia, a really boring baby-sitter who usually stayed in one spot and texted the whole night. Joel settled in with his video games, and when Jelly Bean passed his room on the way to hers, there he was, looking at girls in bathing suits and fancy underwear on his computer. He and his dumb friends were on the phone with each other laughing and making silly comments about each picture. "Ew," said Jelly Bean. "At least shut your door."

She went back down to do some homework at the kitchen table. After that she ate some ice-cream, then lay down on the den carpet near where Pia was sitting, and turned on the TV. The rug smelled like people's feet. Roger-Over dragged himself over to Jelly Bean for her to stroke him. Dr. Pfeiffer was right about Roger-Over not being very hungry. She knew Mom would tell her not to because it was really expensive, but Jelly Bean couldn't help covering Roger-Over with Mom's soft tan blanket that was laying on the chair that was next to her. He stared up at her with a look that Jelly Bean knew meant "thank you."

"Aw," said Jelly Bean, stroking him over the blanket, "sorry you don't feel good, guy. Hey," she jumped up, all of a sudden, "come upstairs with me. I have to do something. You can make it. Yikes," she said, trying to carry him up the stairs. "Come here, Pia. Help me for a minute." Pia rolled her eyes. But Jelly Bean kept calling her until she finally got up to help. "I just have a few more steps to go."

"Are you sure you should be doing this?" asked Pia.

"Yes, I'm positive," said Jelly Bean. "Please!"

"You're the one who's going to hurt your dog," Pia told her. She sounded annoyed. She obviously didn't like being interrupted in her texting.

"No, I'm not," said Jelly Bean. "I'd never hurt him. Would I, Roge?" When Jelly Bean put him down at the top of the stairs, Roger-Over hobbled to Jelly Bean's room, and lay down on her carpet. "Bye bye," she told Pia, shutting her door. Pia made a disgusted face and shook her head.

"I'm just not sure you're supposed to be making him go upstairs," she called to her from outside the door. "You're going to have to get him back down, you know." Jelly Bean heard Pia's footsteps on the stairs go clump clump clump back down. Jelly Bean hadn't thought about that part.

She brushed his coat for a few minutes, then changed into one of her gymnastics leotards. "I have some big decisions to start working on tonight," she told Roge. "You heard what Sam said about deciding on a career. Well, I have to decide whether or not I'm talented enough to start training for the Olympics. That is, if Mom and Dad say it's okay. But I'll have to prove to them I'm serious about becoming a real gymnastics star." She did a handstand and then a handspring. Roger-Over followed her with his eyes and barked.

But when Jelly Bean tried a cartwheel, her room wasn't big enough. She fell and landed on Roger-Over's tail, stubbing her toe on her bed and banging her head on the floor. "Oops! Sorry, guy," she told him. "Ow, that hurt." She rubbed her toe on the side of her bed. "That was pathetic. I should have known this room is much too small for gymnastics. I could have really hurt you, guy. Guess that's it for gymnastics for now. Oh well. I'm going to take a bath." Jelly Bean hobbled to the bathroom and ran the water. "Boo!" she yelled down to Pia, who looked up and even cracked a smile. "I'll be in the bathtub."

"Hey Roge," said Jelly Bean when she was done with her bath, and was wrapped up in her cozy robe. "Did you miss me?" He stopped snoring for a minute and pulled himself over next to her bed. "I know, I look like a big burrito." Jelly Bean picked up "Anne of Green Gables" from the nightstand by her bed, got comfortable lying on her side, and started reading. "Roge, you're the most lovable dog," she told him after a while. Then her eyes were starting to shut, so she put her book on her night table and shut off her light.

Wonder what I ought to be? Jelly Bean thought to herself, as she lay back in bed and shut her eyes. She folded her hands across her stomach. *Sam knows what he wants to be. I need to start thinking about it too,* she thought, feeling herself drifting off to sleep. *I don't know if I could ever be good enough to do gymnastics in the Olympics. So maybe I could try to be an actress...or one of those people who comes in to science classes and explains to the kids all about the animals. But some animals aren't cute like Roge, and I don't want to have to hold the snakes and turtles. Or I could be an astronaut who flies into space to check out other planets. Ms. Peiser told us they're looking for more girls to do jobs in science and technology…no, mom would never let me go into space. Dad would definitely not let me. Maybe I could be a guidance counselor…or a teacher – no, they have to yell too much at the kids who don't behave… or someone who works in a bakery, it always smells so good in there.…or a writer, like Judy Blume…* Finally Jelly Bean drifted off to sleep, even though she felt all confused. She dreamt a jumbled-up dream – mostly because it was hard to think of herself as a grown-up – and she even remembered some parts of it in the morning. It made her chuckle to herself.

Chapter 7

In Which Jelly Bean Has a Great Halloween

Monday was the first rehearsal for the play. Jelly Bean felt like an idiot. While everyone else read their lines and Ms. Peiser told them when and where to move, all she did was stand behind a chair. That was where the ship was going to be on the day of the play.

"You were great Jelly Bean," said Taylor in a mean way, when everyone came back to the classroom from the auditorium after the rehearsal was over. Then she pushed all Jelly Bean's books onto the floor. It was the wrong time for her to do that. Hardly aware of what she was doing, Jelly Bean punched Taylor in the back when she turned around to face front, as hard as she could.

"Ow!" Taylor shouted, turning around in her seat to do something to get back at Jelly Bean.

"Miss Kramer!" Ms. Peiser yelled, as she walked into the classroom, just in time to see what Jelly Bean had done. Except she didn't see what had happened before the punch. "Come up here right now."

Jelly Bean walked up to Ms. Peiser's desk. To her surprise, so did Britney Keller.

"I really don't know what to do about your behavior, Jillian. Nothing seems to help. Is something bothering you? Do I need to send you to Mr. Johnston again?"

"I saw what happened, Ms. Peiser," Britney interrupted. Teachers listened to Britney, probably because she acted more grown-up than any of the other boys and girls. "I don't think you saw Taylor knock all Jelly Bean's books off her desk." She pointed to the heap of Jelly Bean's books and papers that were all over the floor in front of her desk. Ms. Peiser had to look around the side of her own desk to see. See?" she asked. "They're all over the floor."

Jelly Bean looked up and saw Taylor making a mean face at her. She looked back at her with a big smile.

"That's still no excuse for punching someone Britney."

Jelly Bean noticed that Ms. Peiser looked terrible. Her hair was a mess, and her eyes were like two dark blue smudges. She was in the worst mood ever. But she didn't make Jelly Bean go to Mr. Johnston's office. In a disgusted voice she told both girls to go sit down. Then she told the whole class that if she ever saw anyone punching someone again, they were going to have to sit in the office for the rest of the day. She told Jelly Bean and Taylor they were both on probation – whatever that meant. It sounded scary though.

"Who are you going around with next week for Halloween?" Britney asked Jelly Bean when the last bell rang at the end of the day, and everyone scrambled to get their jackets.

"I have no idea," Jelly Bean answered. "I guess with my brother Joel, like last year," she told her after she thought about it for a minute. "I didn't talk about it with anyone this year. At least not yet." The kids in our grade barely talk to me, she felt like adding, in case you haven't noticed. Instead, she said nothing as they stood by the locker room while everyone around them grabbed their jackets and called good-bye to one another.

"Then would you go around with me on Halloween?" Britney asked. At first Jelly Bean thought Britney might be talking to someone behind her.

"Me?" she asked.

"Yes, you silly," Britney said, laughing. "Who does it look like I'm talking to?"

"Sure!" Jelly Bean told her. "That'd be awesome!" And she broke into the biggest smile ever.

"I'll call you later," said Britney, as they pushed open the big heavy school door, walked out to the middle of everyone running around and shouting all around them. Britney got on her bus, and Jelly Bean stood waiting for her ride.

"Jelly Bean," she felt someone calling her and then tapping her on the shoulder. She turned around and found Heather standing right behind her. "Remember?"

"Heather, I don't think we made definite plans," Jelly Bean told her, not feeling like looking at her straight in the eye. She had forgotten about their plans accidentally, but sort of on purpose.

"Thanks a lot," said Heather, standing with her head down. She looked like she was going to cry.

"I'm sorry Heather," said Jelly Bean, even though she wasn't really sorry. Their play-date just hadn't worked out well at all, Jelly Bean thought to herself, even aside from Roger-Over getting hit by a car.

"You're not really sorry, Jelly Bean. I can tell. So don't say you're sorry. It's not nice to lie."

"But Heather, you'd probably have a better time with one of your friends who likes dolls as much as you do."

Heather still stood looking at Jelly Bean like she had done something mean. Jelly Bean didn't know what else to say. Heather had been so nice to her last week, it was true, but Jelly Bean still didn't want to be friends with her.

Luckily just then Heather's mother pulled up, and she got into the car. Jelly Bean didn't say good-bye, and either did Heather. Jelly Bean was happy when they drove off.

Soon Taylor came outside, following Shelby and the other girls who were always tagging along with her. Every few steps each one did some dance moves, like they were trying to copy Beyonce. Then everyone except Taylor started to walk home. Taylor was the only one of that group who didn't live near enough school to walk, or who was going to someone else's house.

"Bye Shel," Taylor called loudly. Shelby must have heard her, but she didn't answer. She didn't even turn around. Instead, she whispered something to one of the girls near her, and they all laughed. "Bye Shel!" Taylor called again, this time even louder, cupping her hands on both sides of her mouth.

"Good-bye," Shelby finally called back, but in an angry voice so it sounded like an insult. Taylor came over to where Jelly Bean stood, and pretended to be kicking her. She made noises like a mean animal.

"Who are you going trick-or-treating with?" Taylor asked, in a nasty voice.

"Britney Keller," Jelly Bean told her.

"Goody for you," said Taylor, taking out her phone to text someone. Or to look like she was. "I'm going with Shelby and Reese and the whole group." Taylor would have to get to the house where they were all meeting right on time, Jelly Bean thought to herself, so they wouldn't leave without her. All of a sudden Jelly Bean felt a little sorry for Taylor, even though she hadn't been nice to her recently at all. Maybe it was because Taylor always had to try so hard.

On the afternoon of Halloween, Mom helped Jelly Bean with her pirate costume. "You look great, honey," said Mom. She tied a dark silk scarf with skulls and crossbones on it around Jelly Bean's neck as a final touch. It fell over her shoulder too. "You look like the real deal!" Mom told her. She handed her the sword she had made out of aluminum foil wrapped around cardboard in the shape of a long triangle. Mom was handy like that. She told Jelly Bean she was glad she was able to make a costume out of materials they had at home. Especially with college tuitions coming up, Mom kept reminding everyone, they had to try hard to cut down on extra expenses.

Michael went by just then and laughed. "Ahoy, matey!" he said, holding up a pencil, pretending to challenge Jelly Bean to a sword fight.

"She'd probably beat you Mike," said Brady, who it seemed was always around now. Mom called him Michael's shadow.

"Bet she'd take you both prisoner," Mom added smiling.

"Think so?" said Michael. "On guard!" he said to Jelly Bean, spinning around quickly to face her. "Aaargh!" he said loudly, in a scary voice.

"Aaaahhhhh!" cried Jelly Bean, grabbing Mom's pants leg and hiding behind her.

"Bye Mom," said Joel. He and his two friends were dressed up as devils. All three of them looked ridiculous, with their red ski masks and pasted on triangle ears poking up.

"Oooooh, I'm scared!" said Michael, hiding from Joel behind Brady. Brady jumped up and down, waving his hands all over the place. Jelly Bean laughed so hard she couldn't stop. Brady didn't care what he had to do to make Michael laugh. He reminded her of one of those crazy comedians on TV who was always falling all over the place. His arms and legs looked like they could have been made of rubber.

"Can you guys see all right?" Mom asked Joel and his friends. It didn't look like they could, since their silly ski masks only had teeny round openings for their eyes.

"Don't worry about us," said one of the little devils as they turned around to walk to the door, then kept bumping into each other on the way out.

"I'm glad I don't have to go trick-or-treating with them this year," said Jelly Bean.

"Will Britney be here soon, honey?" Mom asked.

"She said she'd be here at four-thirty." Jelly Bean sat down on the couch. She was getting tired of waiting. "What did you used to dress up as, when you were little?" Jelly Bean asked Mom.

81

"Well, once I was a princess," said Mom. "Grandma made me a golden cape out of some shiny material, and I carried a wand. And she made me a beautiful crown by decorating a headband with tinsel. Honestly, it looked real. At least I thought it did."

"Sounds like the good witch in *The Wizard of Oz*."

"Yes, it was a lot like that," said Mom. She sat down on the couch, leaned forward and crossed her arms over her legs. She smiled and had a far-off look in her eyes, as if she was remembering times when she was young. "Grandma could make just about anything out of household junk. Once she made me a beautiful butterfly costume, and all the other kids at school were jealous of me. I had shiny, silvery wings, just made out of pieces of cardboard covered in rags that had been painted with leftover house paint. Once I was a ballerina, but I think she borrowed that costume from a neighbor. She learned how to be so creative because our family didn't have much money, especially after Grandpa's business failed. My brother's favorite toy when he was little was a shoebox he pulled around the house by a string."

Jelly Bean liked listening to Mom talk about old times, but now she was really wondering where Britney was. It would be so embarrassing if she didn't show up.

Michael walked into the den from the kitchen, and Brady followed close behind him. "Let's go," Michael said to him. They must have finally gotten tired of eating all the snacks in the house and pretend-fighting with pencils.

"Whereto?" he asked.

"Don't know," said Michael. "Out," he explained.

"Okay boss," said Brady. The two of them were fun to watch, as long as you stayed out of their way. They were always punching and jabbing each other, and neither one of them stood still for very long. Mom said it was all that testosterone that made them act so crazy. She explained it was something that boys had a lot of, especially when they were teenagers.

"Hey, let's go to Cameron's house for a little trick-or-treat," Brady said to Michael on their way out. The storm door slammed shut. Jelly Bean watched out the living room window as Michael smacked Brady on the back, and Brady smacked Michael on his back as soon as he turned around and headed down the sidewalk to where their car was parked. She and Mom watched them pretend-fighting all the way to the car, trying to duck out of each other's way.

This made them laugh really hard. Mom shook her head as she got up and went into the kitchen, where she put her melted cheese back into the microwave.

"The two of them are nuts," said Mom, sighing.

"What do you think Michael's going to be when he grows up?" Jelly Bean asked her.

"I wish I knew," said Mom.

"A bum, most likely," Sam answered. He was sitting at the kitchen table quietly studying.

"Bite your tongue," Mom told him.

The doorbell finally rang, and there was Britney. Her raincoat was belted tightly at the waist, and over it were slung a few long strands of bright orange, yellow and blue beads. She was wearing a large dark green floppy hat slanted down on her forehead, and really high heels that made her wiggle and wobble while she walked. She had smeared on a ton of bright red lipstick, and painted a big brown beauty mark right near her mouth. "How do I look?" she asked as soon as Jelly Bean let her in. She twirled around, and then almost toppled over.

"Great!" said Jelly Bean, not sure what else to say. Then both girls giggled. Mom and Sam stared.

"My goodness," said Mom, looking as surprised as Jelly Bean could ever remember seeing her look. "What are you supposed to be Britney?"

"A street-walker, ma'am," answered Britney, pulling out a long silver cigarette-holder from her pocket, and sticking a real cigarette in it.

"Okay, well have fun girls," said Mom, shaking her head. "And be sure to be back by five-thirty."

"Aw Mom, please six-thirty?" Jelly Bean whined. "It's already five-o'clock!"

"Nice your mom can be home to worry about you," Britney said to her, as she wibble-wobbled down the walk. There was nothing for Jelly Bean to do but skip along right beside her. Britney twirled her beads, and took pretend puffs of her cigarette.

"See you later," Jelly Bean called back to Mom, turning halfway down the walk. When they got to the end of the walk, Dad was pulling into the driveway.

"What have we here?" he asked, leaning out his car window.

"A lady of the night," Britney told him, posing with one hand on her hip, her other hand behind her head. Jelly Bean couldn't stop giggling.

"And one pirate," said Jelly Bean, trying to pose the way she had seen pirates pose in cartoons. Then she saluted Dad, who laughed and blew her a kiss.

"You girls have fun," said Dad, "and don't let any ghosts or goblins get you." He turned around when he pulled up to the garage. "I can drive you around if you want," he offered.

Jelly Bean and Britney looked at each other.

"That's so nice of you," said Britney, taking off one of her shoes to rest her foot.

"Of course, girls," said Dad, as he got his coat and briefcase out of the car and turned to go inside. "I'm going to get a quick bite to eat. Text me in about fifteen minutes and let me know where you are."

Going around with Britney turned out to be the most fun Jelly Bean could ever remember having. Ever. At each house she would strike a funny pose, usually with one arm out, and the other hand behind her head. Then she said "Hello" in a deep funny voice, and asked whoever answered the door if they had any goodies for a pirate and a lady of the night. Grown-ups who answered their doors looked like they weren't exactly sure how to react, but most of them just laughed. If a kid answered, they looked a little confused. Jelly Bean and Britney each got a ton of candy.

"We're a good combination," Britney said to Jelly Bean, and they linked arms. But by now Britney could barely walk. So she took off her high heels and threw them in the grocery bag with her candy. A minute or two later, they both heard a ripping sound, and the bottom of Britney's bag broke wide open. Her candy spilled all over the place. And there was a lot.

"Whoa!" said Britney. They both leaned over, grabbed up all the candy from the street, sidewalk and lawn where it had rolled, and shoved it into Jelly Bean's bag.

Jelly Bean texted Dad and asked him to pick them up.

She told Britney he said to wait right where they were, and he'd just be a few minutes. They were only three streets away from home.

"Your dad's cool," said Britney.

"He's just my dad," said Jelly Bean. She had never really thought of him as cool. It was a funny thought. And soon there he was. She and Britney climbed in the back seat.

Britney rubbed her sore feet. "I don't get how women wear these things," she said, picking up one of the shoes and examining it carefully before throwing it back in the bag with the candy.

They each ate a couple of candy bars, and then decided to save the rest because they had each started to feel a little nauseous.

"I can drop you off home," Dad said to Britney. "Just tell me where you live."

Britney told Dad the name of her street, and where he had to turn.

"I feel sick, Dad," Jelly Bean told him.

"Once I ate some melon that had been out on the counter too long," said Britney as she gathered all her things together and pointed out to Dad which apartment was hers. "Oh my god, was I sick," she told Jelly Bean. They didn't usually come to this part of town. At least not ever that Jelly Bean could remember. Sometimes, though, they drove through here on the way to the train or the highway. "I hope you feel better," Britney told her. "I had fun tonight."

"I did too," said Jelly Bean. "I hope we both feel better," she told her, and they waved good-bye to each other.

Britney looked like she was having trouble dragging everything up the walk to her apartment building – her shoes and all her candy, which she had put in an extra bag that Dad happened to have in the car. But she walked quickly now that her shoes were off, almost skipping, her head bobbing from side to side. Dad said to Jelly Bean it looked like Britney had had a good time.

"Have fun?" Mom called from the kitchen, when Jelly Bean came in.

"I had so much fun, Mom," said Jelly Bean, throwing her bag with all the candy in it on the kitchen table. "But I ate a little too much candy."

"Oh Jilly," said Mom, hugging her, while Jelly Bean leaned into her. "I used to do the exact same thing every Halloween. It's hard not to, isn't it? Halloween was always my favorite holiday." Mom tried to help Jelly Bean take off her jacket, but as soon as she had only one arm out Jelly Bean leaned to the side and grabbed her stomach with both hands.

Jelly Bean groaned. "How are you doing Roge?" she asked, as he limped over to lick her hand. He followed her upstairs. Her jacket was still half-off, trailing behind her.

"Jillian, you need to take your costume off," Mom told her. "Try and get yourself washed up."

"I'll try," Jelly Bean yelled from upstairs. "Unless I pass out first." Sam's door was open. He was lying on his bed, studying. But Sam always made time for her.

"How was trick-or-treating?" he asked.

"Good," said Jelly Bean, plunking down on Sam's bed next to him. They lay next to each other, crosswise, looking up at the ceiling. "Until the other day, I felt like I didn't have a single friend in the whole wide world. Except for Heather, but I had to be friends with her because I had no one else to sit with at lunch. Taylor was being so mean to me, and Heather was the only girl who would talk to me. She's nice but she's a doll-freak."

"She didn't really seem your type," said Sam, leaning on his elbow and looking at Jelly Bean.

"But she was better than no one. Nobody else would be my friend. It was terrible."

"Girls' relationships are awful."

"Even the girls in your grade?"

"Of course!" said Sam. "Everyone knows how girls act towards each other. Any girl I'm friends with spends half her time complaining about the other girls she knows."

"Why are they like that Sam?"

Sam slid off his bed and did a few quick sit-ups on the floor. "Jilly, if I knew the answer to that, I'd write a book and become a millionaire."

"How would you become a millionaire?"

"Because," Sam answered between sit-ups, "everyone would buy my book because they'd want to find out the answers. Girls are just really tough to get along with. They're so emotional."

"How come boys aren't really tough and emotional?"

"They are I guess, but just in different ways. Usually boys are tougher physically."

"Oh," said Jelly Bean. "Taylor's tough in physical ways too."

"Well, I don't really know about her, but for boys it's just how their brains work. Or it could be that 'y' chromosome. People do studies on it. And it's not all guys. Just a lot of them are."

"Anyway, I had so much fun trick-or-treating with Britney. And maybe if Taylor and my old so-called friends hadn't all ditched me, I wouldn't have ended up being friends with Britney. If I had gone trick-or-treating with them,

I would have spent the whole time just trying to keep up with them and laughing at what they said, and I wouldn't have had half as much fun."

"Sometimes one door shuts and anther door opens."

Jelly Bean thought about that for a minute. "I get it Sam," she said. "And thanks for always listening to me."

"You're a great sister."

"You really mean that? Michael and Joel just think I'm annoying."

"They love you."

"Yeah right."

"They really do. They just don't always show it. That's another thing about most guys. They usually don't show their emotions like girls do."

"I better get ready for bed. I ate too much candy before."

"Don't give me any. I'm training."

"For wrestling?"

"Yup. I can't be a chunky-monkey."

"Come on Roge," said Jelly Bean to Roger-Over, who had just hobbled to Sam's door. He stood there waiting for her. "'Night, Sam. You're the best." Jelly Bean hesitated. "Wonder what it would have been like to have a sister," she added.

Sam got up and tousled her hair. "Guess you'll never know. But you got us instead." He flipped over and went back to studying.

"Yup," said Jelly Bean. Having a sister was hard to imagine. Still, no sister could have been more fun to be with than Sam.

Chapter 8

In Which Jelly Bean Learns More about Britney's Life, Which Is so Different Than Her Own. She Also Gets More Hope from Ms. Peiser About Her Part in the Play

All the next week, Jelly Bean's class rehearsed for the play at least an hour and a half each day. Everyone in the elementary school said that Ms. Peiser was trying to put on the best play ever in the history of Riverbend School. Some people said it was because she wanted to be a drama teacher in one of the higher grades one day. For Jelly Bean, the rehearsals were horrible. Each morning she tried to find new excuses to stay home, but Mom was not easy to convince. In fact, she wouldn't budge.

"I feel like I'm going to faint!" Jelly Bean told Mom one morning before school. She slumped over her egg and toast.

"If you still feel that way when you get to school, have the nurse call me. You know you can always reach me."

"You're mean," Jelly Bean told her. "Your own daughter is about to pass out, and you don't even act upset."

"I am upset, Jillian, that you're letting this school play get to you like this. If I let you stay home to avoid this, how are you ever going to learn to put up with the things in life you don't like?"

"I don't know," said Jelly Bean, looking down at the floor, while she waited for her ride. "And I don't care, either. Besides, nobody would miss me. They probably wouldn't even realize I wasn't there."

"Jillian, we've been through this. You know this is not a reason to miss school." Mom almost sounded a little sympathetic.

"I know," Jelly Bean sighed. "But you can't blame a girl for trying. What about tomorrow?" she asked Mom as the carpool pulled up. Mom handed her her lunch and shook her head.

"Give me a hug," said Mom. "Come on silly."

"You're mean," said Jelly Bean. She let Mom hug her, but she refused to hug back.

"I'm going to come over to your house one day when you have a daughter who keeps begging to stay home from school. I want to be there to see what you do. I'll have a good laugh."

"Ha ha," said Jelly Bean, twisting her mouth into a funny position, because she was trying hard to keep looking as miserable as possible. "I'd let her stay home," she yelled to Mom while she walked down the sidewalk to Gale's car. "I'd let her watch TV and play video games all day long." She waved to Mom. "Think about tomorrow!" she called to her from the car. "I'll try you again!" Mom shook her head, rolled her eyes and shut the door. What did she care? Mom didn't have to suffer through boring play rehearsals, looking like a fool. She couldn't possibly understand.

"Austin and Hadley," Ms. Peiser said to the main pilgrim and his pilgrim wife when everyone had settled down in their seats after the pledge, "You really need to begin learning your lines. Practice with a parent a little bit each night, or with someone else who's willing to help you. By next week, you must be able to say your lines without using your script." Jelly Bean groaned to herself.

Things did, though, begin to improve at lunch, when Britney made room for Jelly Bean at her table.

"Who said you could sit here?" Taylor asked loudly, as she passed by Jelly Bean on the way to her seat.

"I did," Britney told her. "What of it?" Britney walked over to where Taylor was sitting, and put her face up close to hers. "Going to make something of it, Alpert?"

Taylor gave Britney an annoyed look, but Britney stared right back at her. She put her hand on one hip and made her eyes look mean and squinty, until finally Taylor looked away.

"Shelby! Shelby!" Taylor stretched her neck and leaned way over at the table to try to get Shelby's attention. Shelby was all the way at the other end of the table. Taylor stood up and almost knocked her chair over. "Wasn't trick-or-treating fun last night? I got tons of candy! You can have some of mine, if you want."

"No thanks. I have plenty of my own," Shelby answered her, with a look that said to Taylor she didn't want to be bothered by her anymore. Then Shelby turned to Britney, who was sitting next to Jelly Bean. "Where did you go last night? I tried calling you, but you didn't pick up. Maybe your ring was off, but I gave up. I figured you didn't want to go with us, or you would have called or texted one of us."

Britney took a bite of her peanut butter and jelly sandwich before she answered. She took a sip of her chocolate milk. "Jelly Bean and I went around together. We had so much fun," she told Shelby. "No one was home at my house, so my neighbor drove me over. Then we went to about a million houses, and got a ton of candy. My poor feet are killing me today."

"She was wearing really high heels," Jelly Bean added. "We did get a lot of candy."

"Any jelly beans?" Taylor yelled across the table.

"Taylor, can you be quiet?" asked Shelby, pushing her chair farther away from her. Everyone else followed her example, and no one would talk to Taylor or even look at her for the whole rest of lunch period.

After lunch Jelly Bean walked back to class with Britney. "I'm not sure what's in the house for dinner tonight," Britney told her.

"What does your mother usually make?" Jelly Bean asked.

"She can't be home anymore after four," said Britney. She swatted some of the really annoying boys out of their way, so they could walk faster. Matteo and Edris were always punching each other in the halls and making pests of themselves.

"Why not?" asked Jelly Bean.

"Because she got a second job waitressing. I can come to her diner and eat if I want. It's the one that's right nearby, right up route 53. I don't really like to, though. It gets boring there. But she makes a boatload of money in tips at this job. It's busy almost all the time. And we need the money." Everyone was all bunched up in the hallway, as usual.

"Boy and girls move!" Mrs. Glass, the vice-principal, called out in her scary booming voice. Everyone skedaddled to their classrooms.

"So what do you make yourself for dinner, when your mom's not home?" Jelly Bean asked.

"Sometimes she leaves me something in the fridge. Or sometimes I just have a can of ravioli," said Britney. "Sometimes I have a bagel. Sometimes cheese and crackers. Depends what's around. And what I'm in the mood for. Sometimes I just like to have a bag of Doritos and a box of raisins. Raisins have a lot of protein, you know."

This was a lot to think about. "Does your mom like being a waitress?" Jelly Bean asked, after a minute or two. "It looks like a hard job to me." Maybe that was the wrong thing to say, Jelly Bean wondered. But she was beginning to see that whatever she said to Britney seemed okay with her.

"She always tells me she wishes she finished school," said Britney. "She wants to go back one day to study to be a lawyer. Right now though, we can't afford it. I hope she gets to do it. Since she had to make my dad leave, now taking care of my sister and me is all on her. And my dad doesn't give us the money he's supposed to." Britney looked down for a minute. "But my mom's a really hard worker. It's because she has to be. And she's not a complainer. She never has been."

Jelly Bean knew she was staring at Britney, but she couldn't make herself look away. Britney's life was so different from hers, even though they lived so close to one another, right in the same town. "Wonder if your dad will ever change?" Jelly Bean finally asked. "I mean if he'll ever get better?" she added.

"I doubt it," said Britney. "But who cares. I'm glad he's gone."

"Oh," said Jelly Bean. They went arm in arm into the little alcove outside the classroom door to talk privately for another minute or two, even though they knew the bell was about to ring.

"I don't know what I'd do without my mom," said Britney. "She's the best. We don't get to spend a lot of time together right now, but one day we will. On Sundays we try to go someplace fun, but it has to be someplace that doesn't cost a lot. Like a park or something. My sister goes too, if she's not busy. My mom says she's sorry she fell for my dad, but she also said that if she hadn't, she wouldn't have my sister and me now. She said we're a gift to her. As soon as she has enough money saved up, we're going to go on a really great vacation. It's going to be a long car-trip. We might drive all the way to California."

"That's far," said Jelly Bean. "I think it would take you a long time to get there."

"That's okay," said Britney. "We'd all be together. And it's fun to look forward to. It would be an adventure." All the other boys and girls went past them, shoving and pushing their way into the classroom.

"Wow," said Jelly Bean. That was a lot to think about.

"Do you want to come over this Saturday?" she asked Britney. They were standing together in the corner of the alcove, ignoring everyone else who was standing around or going to their seats. "I mean, if your mom and your sister aren't going to be home."

"They won't. They both work on Saturdays. Destiny just got a job in the supermarket, but—"

"But what?" Jelly Bean asked. Britney looked serious. "I don't know if I can get a ride to your house."

"My mom or my dad or my brother could probably come pick you up. I'm sure one of them could."

"Then it's a deal," said Britney. She and Jelly Bean held on to each other and jumped up and down, but then they raced into the classroom to get to their seats. They were the last ones to sit down. Jelly Bean was completely out of breath.

The rest of the afternoon, she couldn't keep her mind on school. Instead, she kept trying to imagine what it would be like to eat dinner alone night after night. It was not a fun thought. She couldn't remember a time when that had ever happened. *I'm lucky,* she thought to herself. Her house was usually noisy and her brothers could be annoying and either tease or ignore her a lot of the time; but still, coming home to an empty house seemed like it would be worse. She thought about Roger-Over and how much she loved seeing him when she walked in the door. She thought about his leg, and wondered when it would finally be all better, and he'd be able to run around the yard and chase the squirrels like he used to…

"Jillian!" Ms. Peiser called out, making Jelly Bean jump up in her seat. They were in the middle of social studies. "This is the third time I've called on you this period, and your mind is off in the clouds somewhere. I don't know what's gotten into you. We need to have a talk after class today."

Jelly Bean twirled her hair nervously. She had a knot in her stomach when the bell rang at the end of the day. She walked slowly up to Ms. Peiser's desk.

"Jillian," Ms. Peiser said, and pushed some hair off her forehead. She looked so tired close up like this, as she leaned back in her chair and rubbed the back of her neck. "How many times am I going to have to speak to you about misbehaving? I know you don't want me to call your mother." Ms. Peiser pushed her chair away from her desk, and squinted her eyes at Jelly Bean. Her eye make-up was all smudged. "Do you want to tell me what's going on?"

"I'm sorry Ms. Peiser. I'll start behaving better," Jelly Bean said. She definitely didn't want Ms. Peiser calling Mom. But even though Ms. Peiser asked her to explain, Jelly Bean knew it wouldn't be easy to tell her everything that had been going on. It was all so complicated, and she wouldn't be able to explain anything the right way. She'd just end up being sent to the school psychologist, and everyone would find out and think she was nuts.

"When can I expect this improvement in your behavior?" Ms. Peiser was asking, when Jelly Bean started paying attention to what she was saying again.

"Starting tomorrow," Jelly Bean heard a voice say. The voice turned out to be hers. "But it's not just me," she couldn't help adding. Lots of other kids in the class daydreamed. She noticed a few of them staring out the window every day, like Rami, or doodling all the time, like Harrison Bevel. She was the only one who kept getting caught, she felt like adding. But there was no point in being totally honest with adults. Most of them didn't really want to get too involved.

"What would I do if everyone said that?" Ms. Peiser was asking. She tapped her fingers on her desk, and she didn't look like she was in any mood to listen. She did look like she wanted to be done for the day. Ms. Peiser wasn't the type of teacher you could open up to. On the other hand, Mrs. Daniels, her last year's teacher, always did act like she cared about what was bothering you. "All right, you may go," Ms. Peiser said. "I'll assume tomorrow the new Jillian will be here."

"She will," said Jelly Bean, as she hoisted her backpack on her back and started walking toward the door.

And then a funny thing happened: Ms. Peiser called her back. "Jillian, about the play," she started to say. Jelly Bean turned around. "I know you're disappointed about your part," Ms. Peiser went on. "The play is only three weeks from tomorrow, as you know." Jelly Bean squeezed the straps of her backpack tightly to her sides, and chewed on her lip.

Ms. Peiser looked like she wasn't sure whether or not to keep going. "I don't want to make any promises to you I won't be able to keep." Jelly Bean was trying hard to make sense out of what Ms. Peiser was saying. "But, if Marlowe doesn't know her lines any better by rehearsal on Monday, I'm going to ask you if you'll step in and take over her part. That means you'd be

Marlowe's understudy." Jelly Bean concentrated hard. "Would you like to go ahead and begin learning her lines, Jillian?"

"Wow!" said Jelly Bean. Her heart was pounding like crazy. "I mean yes, I would," she answered, and stared at Ms. Peiser. Had she heard her correctly? She walked quickly – more like skipped – back to Ms. Peiser's desk, to take the script she was holding out to her.

"The lines that belong to the main pilgrim's wife are marked in red."

"Thanks, Ms. Peiser," said Jelly Bean. She couldn't stop smiling.

"Now remember," Ms. Peiser told Jelly Bean sternly, "Marlowe may have learned all her lines by Monday, or at least enough to prove to me she'll be able to have them all memorized by the week before the play. So this is a 'just-in-case' situation."

"I know," said Jelly Bean, stuffing the script into her backpack.

"Be careful with that," said Ms. Peiser, half-frowning and half-smiling.

"Oh, I will be!" said Jelly Bean. "Bye Ms. Peiser." At the door she turned back. "And my behavior is going to be 100% perfect, from now on."

"Well, that's good to hear," said Ms. Peiser, who was sliding papers into her tote-bag. Jelly Bean practically raced down the hall, almost bumping into a few stragglers on her way to the front door.

Chapter 9

In Which Sam and Mom Warn Jelly Bean That She's Probably Learning Marlowe's Part for Nothing, and Uncle Jack Comes Over in a Bad Mood but No One Will Tell Jelly Bean Why

That night after dinner Jelly Bean locked herself in her room with Roger-Over, and went to work learning Marlowe's lines. If there was one skill she had always been good at, it was being able to learn things by heart. She had always been able to memorize any poem – as long as it wasn't too long – telephone numbers, spelling words, and even some words in Spanish she had heard people use.

After about 45 minutes of practicing the lines in front of Roger-Over and her mirror, Sam knocked on her door. "What's going on in here?" he asked. "Top-secret stuff?"

"This is stuff I'm memorizing," Jelly Bean answered, "just in case."

"In case what?" Sam asked.

Jelly Bean explained about Marlowe's lines, and what Ms. Peiser had told her.

"I wouldn't get my hopes up if I were you," said Sam.

"I'm not," said Jelly Bean, throwing the script down on the rug next to her bed. "At least I'm trying not to," she said, looking down.

"Easier said than done," said Sam. He sounded a lot like Dad.

"I do have a chance though," said Jelly Bean, looking over at Sam. She flopped over on her side and reached down to pet Roger-Over. Jelly Bean knew Sam was only trying to be helpful. She turned over, lay on her back and covered her face with her hands. Then like a crazy person she started kicking her legs up and down.

"Don't say I didn't warn you," said Sam, going back to texting someone, "when you're still a dumb old tree." He said the last part exactly like Jelly Bean would have said it. She threw her pillow at him, but he jumped to the side and laughed.

"I know," Jelly Bean pouted. Sam left. Jelly Bean fell off her bed on purpose, and landed on the floor next to Roger-Over. She must have bumped his bad leg, because he yelped and tried to lick his leg where it must have hurt. She petted him, and lay back on her rug. "That's show business," she told Roger-Over, and stuck her face close up to his. Then she picked up the script where it had landed, and went back to memorizing until Mom called her downstairs to come have a snack, if she wanted one before bed.

"Guess who's here?" Sam asked, opening her door, and popping his head into her room.

"Who?" Jelly Bean asked.

"Uncle Jack," said Sam.

"Yay!" yelled Jelly Bean, bouncing up and down on the edge of her bed. The pages of her script went flying, and Roger-Over barked like crazy. Jelly Bean paused for a minute. "Is Suzanne here too?"

"No," said Sam, mysteriously. "And I have a funny feeling about the two of them."

"What do you mean?"

"Uncle Jack just had a long talk with Mom."

"So?" said Jelly Bean. "They're always talking. He's her brother." Jelly Bean went back to bouncing on her bed. "They're just like us, dummy!"

"This was different," said Sam. "And he's not in a good mood at all."

"Uncle Jack?" Jelly Bean asked. He was never in a bad mood. It was one of those things that just didn't happen. "Why is he not in a good mood Sam?"

"Not sure," said Sam. Jelly Bean got up and ran past him out her door.

"Hey!" said Jelly Bean, practically flying down the stairs. Uncle Jack was sitting at the kitchen table with Mom and Dad. "Haven't seen you in a while, stranger!" said Jelly Bean, rushing in and planting her elbows on Uncle Jack's knees.

"Hi, Jilly," said Uncle Jack, ruffling her hair, but not looking or sounding at all like his usual self. He didn't try to do anything goofy with her. He just sat there tapping his foot on the kitchen floor and flipping through a magazine it didn't look like he was really reading.

Dad went back to eating his ice-cream from the carton. Mom got up from the table and put the rest of the dinner dishes from the sink into the dishwasher.

"Jilly, do you want some ice-cream?" she asked. "Or frozen yogurt with some fruit?"

"Okay," said Jelly Bean, putting her face underneath Uncle Jack's. "Is anyone going to tell me what's going on here? Did you flunk out of your dental school or something?"

Uncle Jack leafed through the magazine he was holding one more time, closed it, and slammed his fist down on top of it. Then he stood up. Jelly Bean looked up at him, and it looked like he might have been crying. She stood in his way, and tried to make funny faces. He smiled, but just a tiny smile, not his usual one.

"I have to go." Uncle Jack reached over for his baseball jacket. Jelly Bean put her arm around him, and walked with him to the door, imitating his long steps.

"Can I walk on your feet, just till you get to the door?" she asked.

"Not tonight, Jel," Uncle Jack told her, softly. She folded her arms and stood in front of the door.

"How come you won't tell me what's the matter?"

Uncle Jack put on his baseball cap, tweaked her nose, and opened the front door. He kept looking down.

"What's going on with the play, Jilly?" Mom asked, after Uncle Jack left. Could Mom make it any more obvious she was trying to get her to think about something else?

"I don't want to discuss it." Jelly Bean sat back down at the table. Then she had an idea. "Good night," she said in her happiest voice, grabbing Dad's spoon. "Come on, Roge," she called. He hobbled after her as she ran upstairs.

"Jillian, come back with that!" Mom yelled.

"Not till you tell me what's the matter with Uncle Jack." Jelly Bean slowly came back down the stairs, but she held the spoon tightly behind her back. Mom handed Dad a different spoon and shook her head.

"There's nothing wrong with Uncle Jack, Jilly.   He's just tired," said Mom, falling into a chair at the table and checking her phone. Dad was back to looking at his iPad, now that he had finished the whole container of ice-cream.

"You guys know there's something wrong with Uncle Jack and you just don't want me to know what it is. He never acts that way towards me. Ever.

Either something's the matter with him or he doesn't like me anymore. And either do you guys. No one around here ever wants to tell me anything."

Dad reached over and gave Jelly Bean a big hug. "Sweet girl," he said.

"Hey, that hurt!" said Jelly Bean. "Okay, Dad loves me. But what about you and your brother, Mom?"

"Now you sound silly," said Mom.

"That's not an answer," said Jelly Bean. "And you know it." She tried to look as angry as possible at both of them.

"Jillian," said Mom, "just because someone's tired or not in such a great mood, that doesn't have to mean they don't like you."

Dad looked at Mom, and Mom looked back at Dad. "He's just overwhelmed with all the work he has to do for dental school right now," said Dad. "He also has to study for some tough exams he has coming up in a few weeks."

"Oh," said Jelly Bean, finally.

She threw the spoon back on the table, and yawned. Then she got in the middle of Mom and Dad, and hugged both of them. "Dad, where did all your hair go?" she asked him. "You barely have any left!"

"You're right Jilly," said Dad, turning around to smile at her and Mom. "After paying all the bills for this household, it's no wonder."

"You mean you can't afford us?" asked Jelly Bean.

"Think it's time for you to get to bed, my love," said Mom. Jelly Bean didn't bother arguing. She just yawned.

"'Night guys," said Jelly Bean, feeling gloomy thinking about Uncle Jack as she climbed the stairs. It didn't sound like he was going to be much fun anymore. Roger-Over wasn't even following her upstairs, and she heard Dad saying he needed to take him out one last time.

"Ow! Watch out," Joel yelled at her as she punched him, hard, on her way upstairs. He just happened to be coming downstairs at the same time. To get back, he tried to kick her.

"Hey," said Jelly Bean. "Mom, Joel kicked me," she called.

"Then what did you go and punch me for, idiot?" he asked her.

"Stop it you two," said Mom, from downstairs. She didn't sound pleased.

"She started it," Joel told Mom, in his angriest voice.

"Sorry," Jelly Bean called back, but not like she meant it. She went into her room and shut the door. Jelly Bean flopped on her bed, thinking about how grown-ups never told you anything you really wanted to know. She was tired, but didn't feel like getting ready for bed yet.

Sam opened the door and stuck his head in. "What's the matter?" he asked.

"Nothing," Jelly Bean answered in her unhappiest voice. She flopped over on her side, so she could see Sam in her doorway. "I mean everything." Jelly Bean picked up the script where she had tossed it, but when she tried to read it, she couldn't concentrate at all. And now the pages were all messed up. "Tell me if you find out what's really wrong with Uncle Jack," she said.

"Will do," said Sam. He put his feet together, and saluted.

"Promise?"

"I have a feeling we'll all find out soon," said Sam. "But anyway, you know I always tell you whatever I find out."

"I know," said Jelly Bean. She put down the script. "Thanks Sam."

Mom came in later, when Jelly Bean was ready for bed. She finally told Mom what Ms. Peiser had said to her about the play.

"Don't bother learning all those lines, honey," said Mom. "You'll just end up disappointed."

"I don't care," said Jelly Bean, even though she knew she really would care if Marlowe did come to school knowing her part.

"All right, then do what you think is best." Mom got up from her bed.

"Do you think the dog should be in here all night with her, Bill?" Mom asked, starting trouble again. "There was something on the news that said their fur can harm children's breathing if they're near them for long periods of time."

Dad gave Mom a hug from behind her. "Don't worry so much," he told her, and patted her shoulders.

"Hug!" Jelly Bean called out to Dad. He went to give her a hug, but almost fell over Roger-Over on the way. Mom and Jelly Bean both giggled when Dad acted like he was going to fall down. "You're silly," Jelly Bean told him.

"I'll never let them take you away from me, Roge, I promise," Jelly Bean told him after Mom and Dad left. Ms. Peiser had read the class parts of *Lassie*, and ended by telling everyone that people say dogs are man's best friends because they're so loyal. Jelly Bean understood that feeling.

She drifted off to sleep, thinking how Roger-Over was her best friend in the whole wide world, and that she would write a book one day about all his adventures: how he got run over by a car, how he always listened to her no matter what, and followed her all over the place...then she dreamed she was petting him, and he was looking up at her with his big droopy brown eyes...

Chapter 10

In Which Taylor's Behavior Gets Worse, and Jelly Bean Goes with Dad to the Vet and Roger-Over Gets His Cast Off

On Friday Ms. Peiser reminded the class that they weren't going to have time to rehearse in the auditorium too much during the next week, so they'd have to try to rehearse the best they could in their classroom. After that they all had to go into Mr. Singer's room to watch the skits his students had prepared about famous scientists. Most of the skits were boring, and it also started to get hot and smelly in the room, with so many kids all bunched together. Ms. Peiser left, because it was her free period. A sub was there that day for Mr. Singer, so everyone kept asking to go to the bathroom or to get a drink out in the hall.

The sub, Ms. Alexander, looked young, and she didn't look too happy about what was going on. It seemed like she wasn't sure what to do about it, though.

Taylor was one of the first ones to go out.

When she came back into the room, she had her hand over her mouth but it didn't totally prevent her from laughing out loud. She pushed and squeezed through the crowd of boys and girls until she forced her way to a spot on the floor right next to Shelby.

"Ow!" Isaac screamed out. "You just stepped on my hand!"

"Go away!" Hadley yelled, rubbing her leg that Taylor had pushed against to stop herself from falling.

"That's it," said the sub, in a loud angry voice. "No one else is allowed to leave the room." She told the boy who was performing his skit to stop. He was wearing a gigantic white lab coat, and huge goggles. He was supposed to be Louis Pasteur discovering germs, but he looked like a ghost about to go underwater.

"You're gross," said Shelby, loudly. She jumped up when Taylor whispered something in her ear, and walked quickly to Ms. Peiser, who was just coming back from her time-off. Ms. Peiser bent down to listen to what Shelby was saying. Everyone listened to Shelby. She pointed to Taylor while she talked to Ms. Peiser, using her hand to prevent anyone else from being able to hear what she was saying.

"Everyone quiet down immediately," Ms. Peiser said first. Then she told Brett, whose hands kept getting stuck in his white robe, that he could continue in a minute. "Taylor Alpert, go down to Mr. Johnston's office this minute," she told Taylor. Ms. Peiser held Taylor's arm as she quickly walked her out of the classroom and into the hallway. The whole class started buzzing, and it took poor Ms. Alexander several minutes to quiet everyone down. Then she started screaming, and that finally made everyone quiet down. But a lot of people – especially the boys – were fidgety and couldn't sit still during the rest of the skits.

"I have to tell them never to give me this class again," Jelly Bean heard Ms. Alexander saying to Ms. Peiser, when the bell finally rang.

At lunch, everyone at Shelby's table, including Jelly Bean, had to lean far over to hear what Shelby was saying. She was speaking so softly, she was practically whispering.

"So, she followed Logan Maslow into the bathroom, went into the stall next to her—"

"What's a stall?" someone asked. Shelby rolled her eyes and looked disgusted. Everyone had stopped eating. Luckily Jelly Bean knew what a lot of words meant, which was one of the very best advantages to having three older brothers.

"Then, she stood on the toilet seat, leaned over the top of the wall in-between, and took a picture of her."

"While she was…?" Britney didn't finish asking what she was going to ask.

"Uh-huh," Shelby answered softly. She looked down at her sandwich, and took a small bite. "While she was – you know." She whispered something to Riley and they both giggled.

"Ew!" said everyone at the table, almost in unison. "That's gross," a few people added. People from other tables came over, and then some of the teachers had to come over and tell everyone to go back to their seats. Everyone was talking about Taylor and the picture she took in the bathroom. Mr. Johnston came into the cafeteria with Taylor, and everyone turned around to look.

"Stop," Shelby turned around to say to a group of girls at the table behind them who were giggling. "You sound really immature." They looked at each other, shrugged, and stopped. Ashton Beedle put her head down on Jessie Koff's shoulder, and covered her mouth with her hand. She couldn't stop laughing no matter what anyone said.

"Jelly Bean, you used to be such good friends with her," said Shelby, all of a sudden. Jelly Bean had been in the middle of staring at Ashton and Jessie.

"What?" she said, surprised to hear Shelby say something to her. She wondered how Shelby managed to have everyone glued to everything she said all the time.

"She's not friends with her anymore, Shelby," Britney spoke up, "for your information." Jelly Bean felt like hugging Britney. She was the only person brave enough to talk back to Shelby. People listened to Britney too, even though she was a completely different type of person. "No one knows they're not friends anymore because Jelly Bean's too nice to be mean to anyone," Britney added, loud enough for everyone to hear.

Jelly Bean felt her cheeks getting hot. She wanted to say something, but she couldn't think of exactly what to say that would sound right. Shelby smiled at her, and she smiled back. She thought Shelby hardly knew who she was, aside from her silly nickname. Her heart started beating fast. It felt good to be noticed by Shelby.

Later that afternoon, after gymnastics, Jelly Bean said thanks to Britney for sticking up for her.

"I just wanted everyone to know you're nothing like that brat," Britney told her.

"She used to be nice," said Jelly Bean, as they walked upstairs from the locker room together. "I don't know what happened to her this year."

"My mom says that sometimes people turn on you and start acting mean, just because they want to make themselves feel better," Britney explained. She looked and sounded very serious. Jelly Bean just stood at the top of the stairs. She was concentrating so hard on listening to what Britney was saying that she couldn't even move.

"I never thought about that," said Jelly Bean, still standing there, when she finally figured out what she wanted to say. "It makes me feel worse though, if I'm the one not being nice to someone," she said. And she told Britney all about what had happened when Heather came over on Saturday, and how she had left her alone for a long time.

"But Jel, your dog got run over," said Britney. "She must have understood why you had to leave her alone for a long time."

"No, she was mad at me," Jelly Bean said. "Anyway, my mom told me that Taylor's the way she is because her parents never punish her, and they're both really old. She said they do everything she wants, because they had to wait a long time to have a baby."

"That's the way it goes, I guess," said Britney, pushing her hands deep into her pockets and staring at the floor. "She has two parents and she's the only kid. They pay so much attention to her, and she doesn't even appreciate them."

"They give her everything she wants," said Jelly Bean.

It began to cross her mind that Britney must have felt bad that she only had a mom, and that she had to be at work a lot.

They were quiet together for a little while as they walked outside. "You want a ride home, Britney?" she finally asked, when she saw Mom was about to turn at the light and pull up.

"Not today, thanks anyway Jel," said Britney. "My mom's new boyfriend's picking me up, and we're going to eat dinner at the restaurant where my mom works. She's going to wait on our table."

"That sounds so cool," said Jelly Bean.

"I know. I wish she could be home with me more, but I'm going to do my homework there, and she's going to come over and talk to me when she's on break."

"Have fun," said Jelly Bean, when they heard a car honk, and it zoomed up fast in front of them.

"Guess he's trying to show off," said Britney. "Bye, Jel!" she called as she got into the car. "See you tomorrow."

The car sped off with a loud noise and a big gust of smoke, and Jelly Bean waved back when she saw Britney turn around to wave. Then Mom pulled up and Jelly Bean had a lot to think about. Luckily Mom was on her phone with Grandma, so Jelly Bean had a chance to think things over without having to answer questions from Mom right away – like how was school today and did she have any homework and how did her hair get all messed up.

Saturday Jelly Bean woke up from the howling noise the wind made when it banged against her window.

"Come on, Roge," said Jelly Bean, almost tripping over him, as she tried to locate the top she wanted to wear. She knew it was somewhere in the pile of clothes she had left lying around in a big messy pile the night before. "Today's your big day."

Roger-Over lifted up his head sleepily and barked one sharp bark at her.

"Can't take you out just yet," said Jelly Bean, searching all over the place now for her other sneaker. "It has to be here someplace." She stuck her hand as far as it would go under her bed. "Mom'll kill me if I go outside in my flip-flops. And besides, look at that frost on the window." She stared at the glisten-y patterns that had formed during the night on her window pane. She pushed aside some of the books, papers and clothes on the floor.

"Ta-da!" she called, finding the matching sneaker and putting it on as fast as possible. "Today we go back to Dr. Pfeiffer, Roge." Jelly Bean rubbed the fur on the back of his neck, and Roger-Over licked her and then sneezed a couple of times.

"You get your cast checked today Roge," she told him. Roger-Over put his head back down on his paws and yawned. He was a funny dog. Jelly Bean hoped Dr. Pfeiffer would say his cast could come off.

"Sam!" she yelled, running into the hall.

Roger-Over limped after her, enjoying the challenge of keeping up. "We have to go to Dr. Pfeiffer, remember?" Jelly Bean told Sam, banging on his door.

"Hey!" Michael opened his door – which was right next to Sam's – and stood in his doorway with his hands on his hips, making a mean face. He was wearing a tee shirt that was all ripped up and his pajama pants with black skulls all over them. "Can a guy get some sleep around here? It's the weekend, in case you didn't know." His hair was a big mess, and his eyes were hardly open. His breath smelled awful. But he didn't stand there for long. He stomped back into his room and slammed his door so hard that Jelly Bean jumped.

"You're not up yet?" said Jelly Bean, barging into Sam's room and shaking him.

Sam turned over in bed and squinted up at her. He propped himself up on one shoulder. "Guess what? I told you our band played last night at a big party in the city. It went really well. They kept asking us to stay longer. I made seventy-five bucks," Sam told her. First, he only had one eye open, then he finally opened the other, but just a little.

He fished around on the table next to his bed, and held up some crumpled money.

"Wow," said Jelly Bean. "That's a lot, Sam."

"I didn't get home till three in the morning."

"Whoa," said Jelly Bean. "So are you too tired to go to Dr. Pfeiffer with me?"

"I want to go," said Sam, falling back down on his bed, and throwing the money all around him. "Yeah, I'll go," he said.

"Good," said Jelly Bean. It was always fun going places with Sam. Jelly Bean loved the way he made her feel grown up.

"What time is it?" Sam asked, feeling around on his messy night table for his phone.

"I have to take Roger-Over out Sam," said Jelly Bean.

"It's already 8:30," she told him as soon as she got back. "We're supposed to be there at 9:30."

"Nine-thirty a.m.?" Sam asked her. "I know, I know," he told her. "That was a joke. At least it was meant to be." Sam fell back onto his pillow.

"Ha ha," said Jelly Bean.

"Honestly, I don't know, Jel," Sam told her, flopping back down on his bed. "I'm exhausted, and I have a raging headache."

"That's okay," said Jelly Bean, narrowing her eyes at him, and twisting her mouth to one side. "I understand," she told him. "Come on, Roge. Time to see what Doctor Pfeiffer has to say about you."

"Let me know," Sam called after her. His voice sounded muffled. He was probably already back under his covers.

"All right, dum dum," she called back.

"Shut my door please!" he yelled after her.

When she got downstairs, there was Dad sitting at the kitchen table, drinking his tea and reading the paper. "Mom tells me we have an appointment with Dr. Pfeiffer this morning."

"We do, Dad," said Jelly Bean, giving him a gigantic hug. She almost made him spill his tea all over the place, but he caught his cup just in time. "How did you do that?" Jelly Bean asked him, looking close into Dad's face.

"I'm not sure," said Dad, smiling at her. "But I better not try it again."

"I'm just going to quick get something to eat," said Jelly Bean, grabbing a package of Pop-Tarts from the freezer.

"Mom lets you eat those things?" he asked.

"Joel and Sam do," she told him. Dad shook his head and shrugged.

The whole way to Dr. Pfeiffer's, Roger-Over kept his head out the window. Jelly Bean stuck her head out the window next to Roger-Over, and kept her hand on the back of his neck. His fur felt so soft.

"Is Uncle Jack still going to marry Suzanne?" Jelly Bean decided she might as well try to clear this up. "Please answer me, Dad." Silence. Dad hummed along to the music. Grown-ups were always trying to avoid answering her questions. "Come on, Dad! I have a right to know."

"Honestly, I'm not sure, Jilly. You'll have to ask Mom."

Jelly Bean groaned. "Dad, she tells me even less than you do. You guys treat me like I'm a baby. Like I can't understand anything."

"I don't think anyone knows for sure what's going to happen with Uncle Jack and Suzanne," Dad said, after making her wait forever.

"What's that supposed to mean, Dad? Either he is or he isn't getting married to her. Which is it?"

"It's not always that simple, Jilly."

"What?" said Jelly Bean. "I demand to know why Uncle Jack said he was going to marry Suzanne a few weeks ago, and now maybe he's not. Was he lying?"

"No, he wasn't lying, Jilly. That's not it. Just sometimes things change."

"Now I'm really confused, Dad. My brain's going to explode!"

Dad stopped at a red light and looked at her in the rear-view mirror while he chewed his lip. "To tell you the truth," he added, "I don't exactly know myself what's going on with the two of them."

Jelly Bean sat back against the seat and thought things over. Maybe Uncle Jack wasn't going to marry that awful Suzanne. So there was some hope after all. Although it had been tough to see Uncle Jack looking so unhappy.

This time at Dr. Pfeiffer's lots of dogs were there. There was a ton of loud barking, and the office smelled like a lot of animals had done their business right before they went into the building.

In the examining room, Jelly Bean watched as Dr. Pfieffer removed Roger-Over's cast. Her poor doggie whimpered the whole time, and at one point he let out a yelp.

"Someone's been taking excellent care of this dog," said Dr. Pfeiffer, inspecting Roger-Over's leg. It looked thin and weak compared to the other three. Jelly Bean reached out to touch it.

"Careful," he cautioned her.

"Oops," said Jelly Bean, quickly drawing her hand back.

"I don't think you'd hurt him, but his leg's still going to be a little sore for a while." Dr. Pfeiffer gently raised and lowered Roger-Over's hurt leg. Jelly Bean turned her head so that she could look Roger-Over right in the eye. "He's a very good dog, Jillian," Dr. Pfeiffer said.

"You mean compared to the other dogs that come in here?"

"You'd better believe it. Some of them really carry on. Growl at me, try to bite me. Of course, with certain breeds it's in their genes, similar to the way it is with some people. With others, you can tell it's how they've been treated. Anyway, mutts like yours are generally the sweetest. And I think a lot is due to you." He looked over at Dad and grinned.

"Thanks, Dr. Pfeiffer," said Jelly Bean, raising herself up and down on her toes, and shoving her hands deep into the pockets of her jeans. She looked up at Dad. He patted her back and smiled down at her. Dr. Pfeiffer's compliments were making her feel a little embarrassed.

"He still needs a cast, but a light one this time, just to keep his leg steady. I'll show you how to wrap and unwrap it," said Dr. Pfeiffer, winding an ace bandage around Roger-Over's leg. "You can leave it off for an hour or two each day." Jelly Bean watched carefully. "Where's your brother this morning?"

"Sleeping late today," said Jelly Bean. "His band was playing someplace till late last night," she explained.

Dr. Pfeiffer smiled. "I have two teenagers myself," he told them. "I understand."

Jelly Bean put Roger-Over's leash back on him, and after they said good-bye, she and Dad walked out to the receptionist's desk. The waiting area was noisy, with several dogs barking, and someone's parrot squawking away. On the way out they saw something funny: a big strong-looking policeman holding a tiny little bird in front of him in his giant hands, talking to it. Mrs. Gibbons, the receptionist, gave them an appointment time to come back in two more weeks.

"Glad he's doing all right," said Dad when they got to the car. Jelly Bean climbed into the back seat, and Dad helped Roger-Over get in next to her.

"Yup," said Jelly Bean. "He's almost back to being perfect again." Roger-Over wagged his tail and licked Jelly Bean's arm.

"Think he's trying to show his appreciation," said Dad. He opened the window next to Roger-Over partway, so he could enjoy the ride home with part of his head out the window. Jelly Bean snuggled up against him. Roger-Over made a great pillow.

Chapter 11

In Which Joel Gets Hurt, Michael and Brady Act Crazy with Their Friend
Cameron, Britney Comes Over and Jelly Bean Has so Much Fun with Her

When they got home, Mom told Jelly Bean she was almost ready to take her
to pick up Britney.   But right now, she was busy cleaning off a cut Joel had
gotten on his knee.

"Ew," said Jelly Bean, looking down at Joel's bloody knee. He screamed
like a crazy person when Mom dabbed first-aid cream on it. "Wow, must have
hurt," she said to him.

"Yeah, it hurts," he said, looking up at her with a scowl on his face. "I fell
off my skateboard, in case you're interested."

"I don't think he needs stitches," Mom said, looking up at Dad. Dad came
over and put his arm around Joel's shoulders.

"Should be wearing knee pads and a helmet when you go out on that thing,"
Dad told him.

"He can't," said Jelly Bean, coming to stand near Dad with Roger-Over
following her. "It wouldn't look cool. He doesn't want anyone to laugh at him.
He'd rather get all cut up and make you guys take him for stitches."

"Shut up, you!" said Joel, and tried to reach out to smack her. Jelly Bean
jumped back. Roger-Over yelped. She knew she should feel bad for Joel, and
she did, deep down. But it was hard not to feel jealous when Mom gave him
special attention – even though his knee did look like a nasty bloody mess.
Finally, Joel got up from the kitchen chair and hobbled away, scrunching up
his face and making noises like he was in a lot of pain.

"Does it hurt when you walk on it?" asked Mom.

"Kind of," said Joel. "But I guess I'll be okay." Two minutes later some of
his creepy friends rang the bell. Dustin had about a gazillion pimples, and
Chase always tried to act like he was someone people ought to bow down to.

His hair was all spiky and stupid-looking. When he talked his voice cracked in a funny way.

"Hi boys," Mom called. "Wipe your feet please," she told them, as they were about to barge across the den to look at Joel's knee.

"Sorry," they both said almost at the same time. Joel hobbled upstairs with them. He looked like he was limping more than he really needed to be.

"Come on, Jilly, let's go," said Mom, grabbing her jacket.

"You would have yelled at me if I went skate-boarding with no helmet and no knee-pads," Jelly Bean said to Mom, when they got in the car. "You never yell at Joel about anything."

"Jillian, I don't know why you're always comparing yourself with Joel. He deserves my attention, especially when he's hurt, just as much as you do," said Mom, shaking her head.

"I know," said Jelly Bean, feeling a little ashamed.

"I hope you learn to appreciate your brother one day, Jilly, because it would be much better for you in the future if all of you got along." Mom sounded so unhappy that Jelly Bean just stared down at the floor of the car, and didn't move a muscle. "In some families, brothers and sisters fight a lot when they get to be grown-ups, and that's a sad thing." Jelly Bean could feel Mom looking at her out of the corner of her eye. "You should always be there for one another in the future."

"Okay, I'll try," said Jelly Bean, wondering to herself whether she could really do it. It wouldn't be easy.

Britney was waving from her window when they got to her apartment building, which looked like a big rectangle made up of dark red bricks. Little white doors with broken awnings separated each of the buildings, even though the buildings looked like they were all connected. And each apartment looked exactly like the others on both sides of it. Britney's was number 57, Jelly Bean remembered from when Dad had driven her home after Halloween. Somehow today the whole place looked even more shabby and run-down. The wind had blown papers and bottles and other garbage over the sidewalks and a lot of it had landed in the bushes and up against the buildings.

Some of the windows didn't have any blinds on them, and others had blinds that were crooked. The paint around the doorways and windows was all chipped. Even the trees in front of Britney's building looked like they were shivering in the wind. Then Britney raced to the car, jumped up and down and waved wildly till Mom unlocked the door, and she hopped in. Jelly Bean didn't pay any more attention to where her friend lived.

Jelly Bean had so much fun with Britney that day. They took a long walk, played video games, talked about everyone in the class – including the boys – and decided to be best friends. Doing just about anything with Britney was fun.

"Can Britney sleep over?" Jelly Bean asked Mom, when they went downstairs for dinner.

"I don't see why not," Mom answered. "Britney, honey, why don't you call your mom?"

"Oh, that's okay, I don't need to," said Britney. "She trusts me to look out for myself. She's not going to be home all night anyway. She'll be happy I have someplace to go."

"Oh," said Mom, giving Britney a funny look. "I think I'd feel better if you would at least please text her."

Michael and Brady came in, and put three boxes of pizza on the kitchen table, one on top of the other. Cameron came in with them, but barely looked at anyone and hardly spoke a word. But Jelly Bean was getting used to her. It looked like Mom was too. She even sent a little smile her way.

The boys sat down the wrong way on their chairs, threw the top box open and grabbed at the pizza. Anyone watching them would think they hadn't eaten in years. Michael tipped his head back, opened his mouth and gobbled a slice. So did Brady. They didn't even bother to take paper plates or napkins, till Mom handed them out to everyone. She shook her head. Dad came in, and told Mom he was taking Joel to his soccer game, which was in Greenville. Joel said he thought he'd be able to still play, even though Mom said she didn't think it was a good idea. He said he'd sit on the bench if he had to. Jelly Bean knew he just wanted everyone to notice his big bandage.

At the table, Cameron whispered something to Michael, who was rocking back and forth in his chair. He handed her a piece of pizza from the mushroom pizza box. "Speak up," he said to her. He leaned over and bonked into her hard with his shoulder. "No one can hear you," he told her. She laughed, but then whispered to him that that had really hurt. Everyone heard her say it, so her face turned all red.

"What?" said Brady, loudly. "You said I should speak up?" He and Michael started laughing and they knocked their fists together. The two of them were even louder than usual. Cameron looked like she wished she could disappear. Her hair fell onto her face and she brushed it out of the way. Jelly Bean noticed her hair had pizza sauce on it. Michael and Brady kept bonking into her, Michael on one side, Brady on the other. She looked from one to the other of them, and then tilted her head back to laugh. Those three never stayed still for very long.

Michael let out a loud burp. Mom raised her eyebrows and shook her head. "You're incorrigible," she told him.

"What's that mean?" Jelly Bean asked. Britney draped her arm around Jelly Bean, and they both stared at Michael. The two of them looked at each other and burst out laughing.

"It means there's nothing that can help him," Mom explained.

Michael and Brady went back to pushing Cameron on one side and then the other, which finally made her drop the piece of pizza she was eating and run out of the room. On her way to the front door, she tripped over Roger-Over, who yelped and barked at her like crazy.

"Jelly Bean," said Britney, "your house is the noisiest house I've ever been in."

"Yay!" said Michael, high-five-ing Brady. "I take that as a huge compliment," he told Britney, and gave her a big smile. He held his hands together over his head and shook them.

"Do you think you two should apologize to Cameron?" Mom asked. Just then Sam came down and said he was leaving for his band gig, so Mom turned around to talk to him before he left.

"Nah," Michael was saying. "Cameron'll be back. This is her idea of fun. She's like a puppy dog, right Brades? She always finds her way back." He and Brady laughed. As they got up from the table, they each grabbed a piece of pizza from the last box. They had pizza all over their faces, but that didn't seem to bother them at all.

"Where are you two going now?" asked Mom, standing up. "How about helping me clean all this up?" she nodded in the direction of the table, and put her hands on her hips.

Michael's phone rang. "What?" Everyone could hear Cameron's voice. "Sure, come back if you want to. It's a free country," Michael told her and hung up. He and Brady laughed. Brady was such a good audience – he laughed at everything Michael said and did. Then all of a sudden Michael turned around, grabbed Mom and gave her a big hug.

"Group hug," said Brady, hugging Mom too. Mom giggled. She looked like she was about to get crushed. Jelly Bean and Britney both started laughing, and neither of them could stop. Mom looked like a tiny plant in the middle of two great big trees.

"Where did all the desserts around here go?" Michael asked, breaking away and opening the refrigerator to carefully inspect each shelf.

"There were brownies in there," said Mom, "unless someone ate them." While Michael hunted for the brownies, Mom leaned over him from the side and smoothed his hair. As soon as she stopped, he shook his head all over the place, like Roger-Over did when came in from the rain. "You're impossible," Mom told him, shaking her head, but smiling as she said it. "Okay," she said, "I need to go up to get ready to go out."

"So where *are* you two going?" Mom asked Michael and Brady. A lot of times it seemed like Michael was Mom's favorite. Jelly Bean had discussed this with Sam, and he had said maybe it was true. He had added that he still thought she loved them all, just each one in a different way. Sam understood just about everything in the whole world.

"I don't know, Ma. I really don't know," Michael was saying. Brady went around on the other side of Mom, and he and Michael started pretending they were playing basketball, with Mom in the middle. They kept moving around her, first one way and then the other. Finally, she put her hands on both sides of her head, and told them they were driving her crazy.

"Please don't come back too late," Mom told them. "And whatever you do, make sure you come back in one piece," she added. They acted like they were dribbling a basketball down a court, and Brady made a sudden move, like he was taking the ball away from Michael. When they got to the front door, Michael acted like he had gotten the ball back, and made a shot from a long distance away. Then the door slammed, and there was lots of laughter outside, until the car started up and the two of them took off. Britney and Jelly Bean looked at each other.

"Wow," said Britney. "Lots of energy in those two."

"Uh huh," said Jelly Bean. "How come Cameron always wants to be with them?" she asked Mom.

"She must enjoy being with them," said Mom. "More than that I can't tell you. All right, girls. I'm going up to get ready. Do you want some of the pizza, or would you rather have something different?"

"Thanks, Mrs. Kramer," said Britney. "We can help ourselves. You can go get ready." They each took a piece of pizza to the microwave. "Did you used to smoke?" Britney asked Mom as she was on her way up the stairs. Jelly Bean saw Mom whirl around.

"Yes, I did," Mom answered, sounding flabbergasted. "What makes you ask that?"

"My mom used to smoke too," Britney answered, sounding a lot like a grown-up. "She chews on her nails the same way you do."

"Oh jeeeez," said Mom. "I need to stop doing that. It's not an attractive habit. You're an observant little girl, Britney."

"Everyone tells me that," said Britney. "So I guess it must be true!"

"Have a fun time tonight, girls," said Mom, still looking at Britney in a funny way. "I have to go up. Pia's coming soon."

"Pia again?" Jelly Bean whined. "Couldn't you get Zoe? Or Dana?" Pia was the last person in the world Jelly Bean wanted Britney to have to be with when Mom and Dad went out. "At least they talk to me like a human being," Jelly Bean pouted. "Pia acts like I'm in her way."

"What's the difference, Jel?" Britney asked. "At least you have someone here, in case the house goes on fire, or someone tries to break in. And anyway, you can talk to me. You don't have to pay attention to her at all!"

Mom turned to Jelly Bean on her way upstairs, and gave her a look that said, "I'm glad your friend said it to you, and not me." Then she went upstairs to her room.

"My mom can't afford to hire baby-sitters right now," said Britney. "So I usually stay with my sister. Or I have to go to a neighbor's if she has to go someplace. I guess you know most parents won't let their kids come over to my house." Britney looked down. Jelly Bean didn't know that for an absolute fact, because she had never talked to anyone about Britney. "My mom says she's going to make everything up to my sister and me one day. As soon as she gets back on her feet, and we're not struggling about money anymore."

"Do you ever get scared, I mean when your mom's out?" Jelly Bean asked, biting into her piece of warmed-up pizza.

"Sometimes I do," said Britney. "A little bit. It's usually not for that long though."

Jelly Bean went to get Roger-Over's leash from the laundry room, raced back, and put it on him. "Come on Brit, let's walk the mutt," she said, trying to imitate the way Sam said it. Jelly Bean yelled upstairs to Mom that they were going to walk Roger-Over.

"Maybe we could play one of your Wii games later," Britney said, when they got outside.

Jelly Bean tried to think whether there was some new game lying around that she had forgotten about. "Those are kind of old," she told her.

"They'd be new to me," said Britney. "I don't have any."

"Oh," said Jelly Bean, pulling Roger-Over with all her might. He was trying to chase a gigantic dog that one of the neighbors was walking. Luckily Mr. O'Keefe was holding his dog's leash pretty tight. "Okay, sure, we could play them, Brit," she said, feeling her cheeks get red. Roger-Over was being stubborn. She had to pull on his leash so hard her hand hurt. But she was glad he was making her turn away from Britney, at least for right now.

"Let's go back, Brit," said Jelly Bean. Mr. O'Keefe had finally gotten his dog to go the other way.

"Sorry girls," he yelled over his shoulder at them.

"I'm freezing," said Jelly Bean.

"Do you think I might be able to borrow one or two of your games?" Britney asked as they turned around and starting walking back.

"Sure, take as many as you want," said Jelly Bean. "We don't use them too much anymore." They practically ran back home, not saying much to each other. Jelly Bean hunted around for something else to add, but she couldn't think of any words that would come out right.

Soon after they got home, in walked Pia. She was tall, skinny and stooped over. She wore large round black glasses which kept falling down, and she always looked mopey.

"I left some hot chocolate for you girls," said Mom, on her way out the door. She looked so pretty, and Dad looked handsome – for an old guy, anyway, who was getting really bald.

"Hi Pia," said Jelly Bean. "This is Britney."

"Hi," said Pia, in her voice that had no expression. She didn't even look in their direction. After she settled into one of the kitchen stools, she finally looked up from her magazine and squinted at them. "Nice to know you Britney," she said, sounding like a robot. She pushed up her glasses, picked up her magazine, hunched over and continued reading, kicking her leg up and down the whole time.

116

"How old are you?" Britney asked Pia, while Jelly Bean went into the kitchen and opened a can of dog food for Roger-Over.

Pia looked up from her magazine, and pushed her glasses higher up on her nose. "Sixteen," she answered.

"So's my sister," said Britney. "Maybe you know her."

"Maybe I do," said Pia, and kept on reading.

"Guess you like *People* magazine," said Britney.

Pia looked up. "I should be studying for the SATs," she said, "but I like reading all this stuff about the stars in Hollywood. It's really entertaining." Pia was so hunched over her magazine, she looked like she was going to gobble it up. All the times Pia had baby-sat on Saturday nights, she had never had a conversation with her, Jelly Bean thought to herself. But it seemed as if everyone, no matter how old or young they were, talked to Britney. Pia pushed her glasses up again, and crossed one long bony leg over the other.

"Let's go up," Jelly Bean said to Britney, and they ran upstairs to her room, followed closely by Roger-Over. He started barking like crazy, probably because he still couldn't climb the stairs as fast as he'd like to.

"She's a real live wire," said Britney, plunking down on the guest bed. Jelly Bean plopped down on her bed and they both started laughing. Being silly with Britney was the best.

"What's a live wire anyway?" asked Jelly Bean, when they both finally calmed down. She didn't know what it meant, but it had sounded funny.

"Someone who has a really great personality," Britney answered. They both started laughing again, only this time Jelly Bean needed to grab her tissues because she had been laughing so hard, she had started crying.

"Oh boy," said Jelly Bean. "It's not even that funny, if you think about it," she added.

"I know!" Britney agreed, and they both giggled some more, but this time they calmed down a little more quickly.

"But the laughing part was fun Brit, you have to admit."

"Hey, you're a poet but you don't know it," said Britney.

"Uh-oh," said Jelly Bean, starting to hiccup.

"What's going on in here?" Mom asked, opening the door to Jelly Bean's room. "What's so funny, you two?"

"First shut the door," said Jelly Bean. "I thought you guys had left."

"Just about to," said Mom. "We won't be back late."

"That new?" Jelly Bean asked. Mom looked so pretty, with a bright pink sash tied around the waist of her black dress that had short sleeves and a scoop neck. She also smelled good, although the perfume she had on was making Roger-Over sneeze. Also, her hair was down but kind of puffy, and swished when she walked. Her dress sounded swishy too, and her high heels went "click-click" on Jelly Bean's floor where there was no carpet.

"Britney called Pia a live wire," she told Mom, as they started laughing all over again. Britney came over and put her arm around Jelly Bean when she finally calmed down, and Jelly Bean put her arm around Britney. She hiccupped again, and that made them laugh some more. Jelly Bean thumped her chest, and they both groaned. Roger-Over got up to rest his head on Jelly Bean's knees.

"BFFs?" Britney said to Jelly Bean.

"Works for me!" said Jelly Bean.

"All right girls," said Mom, "please be nice to Pia and don't make her feel bad. She's reliable, and maybe she's not a live wire, but at least I know you'll be safe while Dad and I are out. And don't go to bed too late."

"Good-bye, girls," said Dad, coming to the door behind Mom and putting his hands on her shoulders. "Have fun." He swooped down to give Jelly Bean a big hug and kiss on her forehead.

Then he patted Britney on the head. She smiled and scrunched up her shoulders.

"Bye Dad, bye Mom," said Jelly Bean.

"Let's go play Monopoly," said Britney, as soon as Mom and Dad had left. "I love that game."

"Okay. I mean, I haven't played it in like forever, but I used to like it a lot. Sam used to play it with me."

They went back downstairs, set up the game, put the money in neat piles, and played for a while. Jelly Bean had a few houses, and Britney even had some hotels.

"Do you want to go online? See what everyone's up to on Insta?" Jelly Bean asked.

"I know it sounds nuts, but not really," Britney told her. "All it does is make me feel like I was left out of something fun that everyone else is doing."

"That is true," Jelly Bean said, after she thought about it for a second or two. Even Pia looked up and stared at Britney for a minute, before she went back to reading and chewing on her nails.

Chapter 12

In Which Uncle Jack Comes Over Unexpectedly While Mom
and Dad Are Out. Something Unusual Happens

"We could play cards, if you want."

"You mean online?" Jelly Bean asked.

"No, silly! Real cards."

"Think I know where some are," said Jelly Bean. "I used to play gin rummy with my grandpa, when I was younger. He's really good at cards."

"So was my dad," said Britney in a quiet voice. She pursed her lips together and looked down.

Jelly Bean thought she heard noises outside. "Did you hear that?" she asked Britney.

"Might have," said Britney, carefully putting all the pieces back in the Monopoly box, even though Jelly Bean told her she could just throw everything back into the box. "Could be your brothers."

Now Jelly Bean was sure she had heard strange noises coming from outside. It didn't sound like either Michael, Sam or Joel. "Pia, did you hear that?" she asked, sprinting down the stairs with Britney to the kitchen.

Pia looked up from her magazine and pushed back her glasses. She crunched on some potato chips. "Hear what?"

Jelly Bean and Britney looked at each other and rolled their eyes. Jelly Bean looked at Britney and rolled her eyes some more, but she was getting scared. Roger-Over came down to the front door and barked like a maniac at whoever was coming closer and closer. The noises were getting louder, and now they were right outside the door.

The doorbell rang.

Pia looked up. "Are you guys expecting anyone?" she asked.

"My mom would have said something," Jelly Bean answered.

"Think I should call the police?" Pia asked.

"Jilly, it's me, Uncle Jack," a voice from the other side of the door called.

"Uncle Jack!" cried Jelly Bean, unlocking the door and opening it. "I didn't know you were coming."

"Yeah, I didn't know I was either," said Uncle Jack, in a thick and blurry voice that didn't sound like him at all, as he practically fell forward into the house. Two of his friends were holding him up, one on each side of him. His breath smelled weird and kind of sugary, but also sort of like medicine. He looked like he was half-awake and half-asleep. His hair and clothes were all lopsided too. He was looking at Jelly Bean with a silly grin.

"Where can we put him?" one of Uncle Jack's friends asked. Jelly Bean recognized his friend Henry, but not the one who was talking.

Jelly Bean looked at Britney. She was confused. Pia had gotten up from her seat at the kitchen table, even though she was still holding her magazine. She stood an inch or two behind Jelly Bean and Britney. They all stared at Uncle Jack. Jelly Bean didn't know what to say. Roger-Over was growling at Uncle Jack's friends. Jelly Bean held onto his collar.

"On the couch, I guess," said Britney. She was the only one who was calm and seemed to know what to do and say.

"Who is that?" asked Pia.

"It's her uncle," said Britney. She turned to Jelly Bean. "He's pretty wrecked. You know, drunk," she told her, and when Jelly Bean looked confused, Britney put her arm around her friend.

"Um, we're going to get going, if that's okay," said Henry.

"We, uh, left our girlfriends at the party," said the other friend, whose name, it turned out, was Alec.

All Jelly Bean could do was stare at Uncle Jack, with her mouth wide open.

"Your parents coming back soon, do you think?" Alec asked.

"Um—" said Jelly Bean. She shifted from one foot to the other, looking from Henry to Alec and back again.

"It's okay. We'll be all right," Britney told them. Jelly Bean stared at her.

"Um, I'm not too sure about this," said Pia, taking a step towards Alec and Henry. Uncle Jack was lying on the couch, or more like half-lying there, one arm over his forehead, the other arm slung onto the floor. He closed his eyes and groaned. His hair was sticking up all funny and his good clothes were wrinkly and twisted all over the place. He looked awful.

"We'll let him sleep it off," said Britney to Alec and Henry. "Don't worry. You can go back to your girlfriends."

"You'll be okay, Jack. It looks like you're in good hands," said Henry, going over to him and patting him on the shoulder. "Take care, buddy. We'll check up on you tomorrow."

"Sleep it off," said Alec. "The girls are waiting for us back at Dean's, so we have to go. Sherri'll have a fit. You know how that goes."

So this is what it meant to be drunk, thought Jelly Bean. She had heard it mentioned, but never actually seen an example. Her heart was pounding away. It was scary to see Uncle Jack this way.

"Don't worry, Jel," said Britney. "He's going to be okay. He's not even fully passed out. I don't think we have to call 9-1-1 or anything like that."

Uncle Jack moaned. Roger-Over wouldn't stop sniffing him. He was all sweaty and he did smell weird. He didn't fall asleep, but just lay there on the couch looking like the old Raggedy Ann doll that had belonged to Mom when she was little. His legs and arms were all over the place.

Jelly Bean and Britney stood there looking at him. "Suzanne," he started to moan. "Where's Suzanne?" he said, and wouldn't stop saying that.

"Who's Suzanne?" Britney asked Jelly Bean.

"She's the girl he's going to marry," said Jelly Bean. Uncle Jack groaned. Pia stared at him, and took her glasses off. She looked like she might throw up.

"Do you have any coffee? That'd sober him up before your parents get home," Britney suggested.

"I'll go look," said Jelly Bean. "My parents drink it, so it has to be around here someplace." She didn't have to look very far. The container was right on the kitchen counter. "Found it," Jelly Bean announced proudly.

"Pia, can you help us?" Britney asked. "I'm not sure I know how to work this kind of coffee maker. We have one that's much older."

The doorbell rang. Henry and Alec were back. They were both panting like they were out of breath. "How's he doing?" Henry asked. "We explained everything to the girls – the party's just a couple of blocks away – and they said we shouldn't have left him here with you girls." They looked at each other. Alec took out a handkerchief and wiped his brow. Henry crossed his arms over his chest.

"They said we must be nuts," Henry added. The two of them stood there looking like they weren't sure what to do next.

"Can you help us make coffee?" Britney asked.

"Uh, sure," said Alec. "This guy would be useless though," he said pointing to Henry. "He goes to Starbucks every day for his." Alec went into the kitchen with Britney. Pia went back to reading her magazine.

"What happened to him?" Jelly Bean asked Henry, who had kneeled down to pet Roger-Over. Every few seconds Jelly Bean kept looking over at Uncle Jack all sprawled out on the couch. It was hard to look away. Now his eyes were shut and he was groaning. Roger-Over just stood in front of Uncle Jack, staring and sniffing him. Henry changed his position to sitting cross-legged on the floor by Roge and continued petting him. After a few minutes Roger-Over lost interest in sniffing Uncle Jack and wandered to the other side of the den and lay down.

"Something happened that got your uncle upset," said Alec, turning around where he stood in the kitchen, while he sealed the bag of coffee back up.

"What was it?" Jelly Bean asked, after a minute.   What could have happened to Uncle Jack to make him decide to get drunk?

"Ditched by some broad?" asked Britney, putting her arm around Jelly Bean's shoulders. Henry and Alec looked at each other and then both of them stared at Britney. Alec almost dropped the measuring cup full of water he was about to pour into the coffee-maker.

"Yes, as a matter of fact," said Alec, finally. "That *is* what happened." They both looked over at Uncle Jack and shook their heads. Henry took out his phone to text someone.

"Uh, will you girls be okay?" Alec asked. Henry looked up.

"I guess so," said Jelly Bean, even though she wasn't sure at all.

Pia just stared at them as they headed out the door.

"Your uncle just needs to sleep it off," Britney told Jelly Bean after Alec and Henry left.

"Let's go get a snack," said Jelly Bean. "Do you want to make some popcorn?"

"Ooooooh," said Britney, "good idea." They went into the kitchen where Pia was on the stool in the corner by the stove, looking miserable as ever. She was chewing one of her nails. Jelly Bean took out the popcorn to pop, but by mistake she cut off the whole top of the package, so kernels spilled all over the floor. Roger-Over ran in when he heard the clatter, and started trying to eat them all off the floor.

"Yikes," said Jelly Bean. "Hold him! He could get sick if he eats all this."

"You better hold him, Jel. I don't have a dog, so I'm not so great with them. Spills I can clean up easily. I do that all the time. I'm practically the one-man clean-up committee at my house." Britney found the electric sweeper in the kitchen closet, and quickly vacuumed up the mess. Its loud "vroom" made Roger-Over bark like a maniac.

"I'm getting out of here," said Pia. But almost as soon as Pia shuffled into the den, even over the sound of the vacuum, Jelly Bean and Britney heard screaming. It was Pia. "Help! Help!" she yelled. Jelly Bean and Britney ran into the den. Uncle Jack had woken up and gotten himself off the couch, and now he was chasing Pia all over the den, through the kitchen, then through Dad's cluttered-up study and back again, round and round. Her glasses had fallen off, and her magazine was lying open in the middle of the room. Roger-Over broke away from Jelly Bean in the kitchen where she was trying to hold him, and ran as fast as he could go with his soft cast on, after Uncle Jack. The three of them kept circling around the house like two insane people followed by a crazy animal. "Don't just stand there, get him away from me, you two," Pia yelled at Jelly Bean and Britney. "Make him go away!"

"Come on," Jelly Bean called out to Britney, but even though she and Britney chased after Uncle Jack, they couldn't manage to catch him. For someone who was practically asleep on the couch a few seconds ago, he could sure run fast.

"Suzanne," Uncle Jack was calling as he ran after Pia, "Suzanne! Come back!"

"I'm not Suzanne," Pia shouted. "Girls," she yelled, "get him to stop!" Jelly Bean had never seen Pia move so fast.

"What do you think we're trying to do?" asked Jelly Bean, huffing and puffing. She reached out and now she could just about grab the back of Uncle Jack's shirt.

"I can't believe a drunk person could run so fast," said Britney. "Maybe it was the coffee that woke him up." And sure enough, there was the cup of coffee at the edge of the den table that toppled over when Uncle Jack rounded the side of the table, as he tried to grab Pia.

"Don't go with him!" Uncle Jack called.

"Leave me alone, you lunatic!" Pia yelled. But just as Jelly Bean and Britney had almost caught up with him, Uncle Jack tripped over the cord of the den lamp Mom had just bought. The lamp came crashing down, and broke all over the rug in a thousand pieces of yellow and green tinkling glass.

Uncle Jack lay sprawled out on his stomach on the floor, with blood trickling from a cut on his finger.

"Oh brother," said Pia, wiping her forehead and plunking down on one of the chairs in the den. Her hair was all messed up, and her face was sweaty and red. She blew her nose and wiped tears from her eyes. Then she picked up her glasses and tried to put them back together. "How was I supposed to know this job included being chased around by a drunken nut-job?" She covered her eyes and looked like she was going to cry some more. Instead, she put back on her glasses which she kept trying to fix. But they kept breaking apart all over again. She looked miserable.

"Can you help us clean up the glass, Pia?" Britney asked.

"All right," said Pia, but she didn't sound too anxious.

"You guys have something to clean this up with?" She gave them angry looks when they looked over at her. Britney found a dustpan and broom in the kitchen closet by the door down to the basement.

With Britney in charge, they had everything cleaned up in no time. "Told you I was great at cleaning up messes," she said. "I'll find something to wrap his finger up with." She went into the kitchen and came back with a dish towel.

Luckily Roger-Over wasn't interested in the broken glass.

Instead, he kept sniffing and licking Uncle Jack as he lay on the couch, not moving at all. He looked pretty comfortable down there, with his clothes and hair a big mess, and his head resting on his arm.

"I wonder what my mom's going to say about all this," said Jelly Bean. "Ow," she said, accidentally touching a teeny piece of glass on the carpet. At least the lamp was mostly cleaned up, but now Britney was scrubbing away at the gigantic spot on the rug where coffee had spilled. She was dunking a rag in a bucket of soapy water she had set up. Pia wasn't helping at all. She was reading a different magazine. She had to hold it close up since now her glasses were broken.

"If you think this is bad," said Britney, "you should have seen some of the accidents that happened at our house when my dad used to come in drunk."

"Like what?" asked Jelly Bean.

"Oh, like when he smashed some of the windows with a baseball bat. He also put his fist through one of the doors every once in a while. Once he beat in my mom's car windshield."

"Yikes, that's scary," said Jelly Bean. She stared at Britney. "I would have been scared to death."

"Yeah," said Britney, "I was, pretty much. People do all kinds of weird stuff when they get drunk. I'm never going to drink."

"Me either," said Jelly Bean, even though it was something she had never really thought about. Britney dumped the glass pieces into the kitchen garbage. They made a loud crashing noise. "You could've helped us, you know," she said to Pia, who was sitting on her stool, hugging herself, shaking her head from side to side.

"I don't think so," she said. "Not after your uncle, or whoever that madman is, chased me all over the place. My pay grade isn't high enough to take all that abuse."

Jelly Bean looked at Britney, and Britney looked at Jelly Bean. She shrugged. "Hey, let's make that popcorn," she said.

"Let's!" said Britney. "I'm hungry." They both peeked around the corner of the kitchen to look at Uncle Jack. He was fast asleep. His mouth was wide open. Roger-Over was curled up next to him. He must have been waiting for the next running and chasing game he was going to play. It must have been the most fun he had had in a long time.

"I never knew someone could snore that loud," said Jelly Bean. "He sounds like a train coming through."

"It is pretty loud," Britney agreed. "He looks okay though. He should be fine in the morning."

"Thank goodness you were here," said Jelly Bean. She stood on the step stool and took down another package of popcorn. "I don't know what I would have done." She stuck it in the microwave.

"Can you guys please be careful with that?" Pia said. "I've had more than enough excitement for one night." She twisted up her mouth.

"You want some?" Britney asked.

Pia just shook her head and frowned. "Well, maybe I'll have a little," she said. "If you guarantee that no weirdo's going to start chasing me all over your house again." They looked at each other, and then the popcorn was ready, so Britney handed Pia a bowl.

"You've suffered enough tonight," Britney told her. "And anyway, you'll be glad to know he's out cold." Britney was full of surprises. She was like an adult in a lot of ways, but like a fun adult.

"Uncle Jack used to be so nice to me," Jelly Bean said to Britney, while they were eating their popcorn from the large bowl in the kitchen. "He used to be like a really special friend, you know? Then as soon as he got his girlfriend, everything changed. Her name was Suzanne, but I guess you figured that part out."

Britney nodded. "Do you have any seltzer?" she asked.

Jelly Bean got up and poured some for both of them. "After he met her," she went on, "he didn't have time to do anything with me anymore."

"I do know what you mean," said Britney, scooping up some more popcorn, leaning her head back, and shoving it into her mouth. "Well," she added, "at least it's not your mom who gets mixed up with new guys who aren't always so nice to you. My mom had some really crazy boyfriends."

"Wow, that would be a lot worse," said Jelly Bean. "I don't know what I'd do if my mom did that." She stared at Britney for a few minutes. "Why does she?" she asked, finally.

Britney shrugged. "I think it's because she's lonely," she answered, looking away. "When she was younger a lot of guys wanted to be with her. But she says now it's hard to find a good guy, because she's older."

"Oh," said Jelly Bean, still not exactly sure why someone's mom would get mixed up with boyfriends who weren't nice. "Let's get into our pajamas," she said.

They got ready for bed and were sitting on their beds talking with the lights out, when they heard the garage go up.

"Uh oh," said Jelly Bean. "Now they're going to see him."

"You knew that was going to happen," said Britney. Jelly Bean and Britney stood at the top of the stairs.

"I know," Jelly Bean whispered. "I just feel bad for my mom and all. And for my uncle."

"I wonder what's wrong with Jack?" From the top of the stairs, they watched Mom go over to him and lean down to stroke his forehead. "Pia," they heard her say, "why is my brother here? What happened?"

Jelly Bean and Britney stood where they were and listened to Pia explain what Uncle Jack had done, including the part about chasing her around the house. Then Dad said he'd better drive Pia home. But Pia said she'd rather walk, and that she couldn't come to this house any more. Mom took out some money, and Dad and Mom both apologized to her a couple of times each.

"Hi Mom," said Jelly Bean, coming to the bottom of the stairs with Britney after Pia left. "Hi Dad."

"Hi, Mrs. Kramer," said Britney. They both scrambled over to Mom, who looked like she was stuck leaning over Uncle Jack. She said something in a low voice in his ear that Jelly Bean couldn't make out, and Uncle Jack moved around and started to wake up. He twisted his face in a funny way and stretched. Then he leaned over on his side and groaned. He rubbed one eye for a little while. Roger-Over went over to Uncle Jack's face and tried to lick it, but Mom pulled him away and told him not to. She sounded upset.

"I'm not sure I want to know the answer," Mom asked, "but what happened to my new lamp?" She stood with her hands on her hips and shut her eyes.

Jelly Bean and Britney explained what happened, including how it got there, and especially the part about Uncle Jack chasing Pia around and calling her Suzanne. Mom's eyes opened wide and she wrinkled up her forehead. One good thing was that Pia wouldn't be coming to baby-sit anymore. Uncle Jack looked like he had fallen back to sleep again. The doorbell rang.

"Oh my goodness, I forgot!" Mom said, laughing, when she went to open the door, and their friends the Haleys walked in.

"Sandy, are you okay?" Mrs. Haley asked. "We've been standing out there. Did you forget about us already?"

"Apparently it's been quite a night here," said Mom, slapping her hand to her forehead.

"That's all right," said Mr. Haley, who looked really old – especially compared to Mom and Mrs. Haley. Maybe it was because he was mostly bald but the hair he had left was all white. He had a big fat belly too. "We can come over for dessert some other time if it'd be better for you," he told Mom and Dad in a booming voice. The place did look a mess, especially with Uncle Jack sprawled out on the den floor.

"No, it's really fine," said Mom. Dad went into the kitchen to start getting out the desserts. "Of course we still want to have you.   I bought all sorts of cake Bill," she called to Dad. "It's on the bottom shelf of the fridge in the back." Jelly Bean had seen the cake boxes, but figured she wasn't supposed to open them.

128

"Ooh," said Jelly Bean, "I was wondering what was in those," she said to Mom. She and Britney decided to hang around the kitchen.

"Sounds like you girls had your hands full tonight," Mom said to Jelly Bean and Britney, and looked at them with one of her eyebrows raised up. "Listen," she told Mrs. Haley, turning to her, "it looks like my brother came here after getting himself drunk tonight." She handed the big bowl of grapes and cut-up melon to Mrs. Haley and asked her to please put it on the table.

"We don't have to stay, Sandy," Mrs. Haley said again. Jelly Bean never knew what to say to Mrs. Haley, who was one of those adults who stared at her a lot. Mom had once told Jelly Bean that the Haleys had had one child, but he was born with a lot of things wrong with him. It had sounded mysterious and Mom would never talk anymore about it, but still being stared at made Jelly Bean feel weird. But Mom had also told her that the Haleys couldn't have any more children after that one, even though Jelly Bean had once overheard Dad say he didn't understand why they didn't adopt a child who needed a home. Mom had told him they must have had their reasons. So there were the Haleys, both staring at Jelly Bean and now at Britney too, and there wasn't much she could do about it. She tried to smile at them both, but she didn't really feel like it. And Jelly Bean wanted to wait around for Mom to open those dessert boxes. Britney kept eyeing them too.

"There," said Mom, putting some special cookies and brownies from the box on the dining room table. Phew, thought Jelly Bean, good thing she hadn't opened up those boxes. It would have been embarrassing. "Britney," said Mom, turning to her, "I'm sorry you had to be here when this happened to Jillian's uncle. It must have been scary for you girls."

"No sweat for me," said Britney, before Jelly Bean had a chance to say anything. "I felt kind of bad for him, being ditched by his girlfriend and all." Mom stopped what she was doing, and stood completely still for a minute or two. She stared at Britney with a strange expression on her face. Mom always looked like she wasn't exactly sure how to respond to Britney. This time she looked surprised, and not in an especially good way. Mrs. Haley also stood still on her way back from the dining room to the kitchen. She and Mom looked at each other.

After the grown-ups went to sit down, Mom looked across the table at Mrs. Haley, and Mrs. Haley looked back at Mom. Jelly Bean and Britney stood between the entrance to the dining room and the den, where they could see the grown-ups in front of them, and Uncle Jack if they turned around a little bit the other way. Mom didn't look too happy, and either did Mrs. Haley. Mom actually looked like she felt a little sick.

"Please, everyone, take some fruit and cake," she said. The men dug in.

"There goes my diet," said Mr. Haley, even though it looked like it had gone a long time ago.

Mom looked over in Uncle Jack's direction. She cleared her throat. "I don't want you to think," she finally said, with a big sigh, "that uh, this kind of thing happens around here all the time." Mrs. Haley was spending a long time looking down at the middle of the table deciding what desserts to choose. "I mean," she said, "I think it's just that…" Dad cleared his throat and looked like he was trying to think of something to say to help her finish the end of her sentence.

"Oh, it's okay," said Britney, causing the adults to all turn around to stare at her. "Sometimes people get drunk. It's nothing that unusual. It wasn't like he was a mean drunk or anything. Just went a little crazy." She looked at Jelly Bean, who looked over at Mom. "He did chase around your baby-sitter for a while," she added. "He was probably just having a bad night."

Mom's forehead wrinkled up. She sat back in her chair and crossed her arms over her chest. "Well," she said, looking over at Dad. Poor Dad, he looked like he felt bad for her that this was all happening in front of their friends.

"It's true what Pia said Mom," said Jelly Bean. "He was chasing her all over the place," Jelly Bean told her. "That's how the lamp broke. Uncle Jack tripped over it while he was running. It was kind of funny. Well, it was a little scary while it was happening. I never did see Pia move so fast." She and Britney looked at each other and giggled.

"That's one way to get rid of your baby-sitter," Britney said to Jelly Bean, and they laughed even more. They put their arms around each other, and Jelly Bean laid her head on Britney's shoulder. Britney was the best friend a girl could ever wish for, Jelly Bean decided.

Mom shook her head. She gave Mrs. Haley a confused kind of look, and twisted her mouth from one side to the other. Then she excused herself and went into the den to take a look at Uncle Jack. He was fast asleep now on his side with both hands tucked underneath the side of his head. At some point he must have climbed up on to the couch. He looked peaceful, with his mouth wide open, just gently snoring away.

"Son of a gun," Mom said to no one in particular, staring down at Uncle Jack. "Go figure," she said to Mrs. Haley who had come to stand next to her, and put her arm on Mom's shoulder. They looked at each other, and both shook their heads. Dad and Mr. Haley came in to look too, like they were looking at one of those display cases in a museum. Dad folded his arms across his chest.

"He honestly wasn't acting that terrible, Mrs. Kramer," said Britney.

Jelly Bean and Britney came into the den and sat down cross-legged on the floor right by Roger-Over. "Thank goodness you were here, Brit," said Jelly Bean, as they both petted him. "I don't know what I would have done." When she looked over at Mom, she was making that funny face again.

"Could still be some glass there, Jel," said Britney.

"Ooh, you're right," said Jelly Bean, springing up fast.

"Well, let's leave him be and go into the dining room and have dessert," said Mom.

"Can we take some upstairs?" Jelly Bean asked, going into the dining room with Britney. She leaned over Mom when she sat down.

"Yes you may," said Mom. She looked exhausted. She put some of the brownies and cookies and fruit on a plate, and handed it to Jelly Bean and Britney. "Here you go girls."

"Looks yummy," said Mrs. Haley.

"Can't believe my brother gets rid of my baby-sitter and my new lamp, all in a night's work," Jelly Bean heard Mom say to Mrs. Haley as she and Britney walked faster and faster and then ran to the stairs with their desserts.

"Did I ever tell you about *my* lunatic of a brother?" Mr. Haley was saying to Dad, as Jelly Bean and Britney stood at the top of the stairs and gobbled up their desserts. They looked at each other with their eyes opened up wide.

"No, I don't think you ever did," said Dad. "I don't remember you ever mentioning a brother."

"Well," said Mr. Haley, as the girls tiptoed back down to the kitchen to put the empty plate in the sink, "it's a long story. He's actually a half-brother, and has something of a criminal record."

"Is that so?" Dad answered, sounding as if he was trying hard to concentrate on what Mr. Haley was saying.

Jelly Bean and Britney stood completely still by the kitchen sink, and covered their mouths with their hands so they wouldn't laugh out loud.

"Yup," said Mr. Haley, taking a sip of his coffee. "He's been incarcerated a time or two."

Mom must have heard Jelly Bean and Britney hanging around in the kitchen, because they heard her push out her chair and get up. They scrambled upstairs, got washed up in the bathroom and kept the water running so the grownups couldn't hear their loud giggles. Then they ran to Jelly Bean's room and jumped into their beds. Having Britney over was the most fun Jelly Bean could ever imagine. Roger-Over followed them in and lay down in the middle of the two beds. They each bent over to pet him.

"He's so soft," said Britney.

"I know," said Jelly Bean. "I wonder when Uncle Jack's going to wake up."

"Probably in a couple of hours or so," said Britney. "Wonder if he'll remember what happened."

"You really think he might not?" Jelly Bean asked.

"After they get drunk, some people do remember, and some people don't. Most people say they don't."

Jelly Bean thought about that. "I wonder why?" she asked.

"I don't know," said Britney. "It's just what happens to people when they drink."

"We got to be best friends just in time," Jelly Bean told Britney. "If you hadn't been here, I would have completely freaked. It's not like Pia's the most helpful person in the world."

"I guess the good news is you won't have to be seeing much of that live wire anymore," said Britney. Both girls laughed.

They heard Dad coming up the stairs.

"Good night, sweet girl," he said, sitting down on Jelly Bean's bed. He leaned over to give her a big hug. "Thanks for helping out here tonight," he said to Britney.

"You're welcome," said Britney. "It was an interesting night," she went on. "If you like drama, that is." Dad just smiled and went back downstairs. Jelly Bean thought that Britney must have been a little sad that she didn't have a nice dad to come say good night to her.

They lay there for a while quietly, each petting Roger-Over. "Brit –" said Jelly Bean, finally.

"I know what you're going to say," said Britney. "Don't worry about me," she said in a soft voice. "I'm okay. I'm really glad we're friends, Jel."

"I am too," said Jelly Bean. She wasn't sure what else to say to Britney, so she stared up at the ceiling for a while. "Good night, Brit," she said, finally.

"'Night Jel," said Britney. They reached across the space in between the beds to hold hands for a minute or two. Then Jelly Bean mushed up her pillow and fell fast asleep not too long after that, thinking about all the strange things that had happened that night, and how awesome it was having Britney there.

Chapter 13

In Which Jelly Bean Memorizes All Marlowe's Lines, Britney's an Awesome Friend, and Sam Explains to Her What Happened to Uncle Jack the Night Before

When Jelly Bean and Britney came downstairs on Sunday Uncle Jack was up, but he wasn't in a good mood at all. He was standing in the kitchen with an awful expression on his face, and he looked like he didn't feel very good. Mom was offering him all different kinds of food, but he kept saying no to everything, and told her he wasn't hungry. Uncle Jack usually ate just about everything that wasn't nailed down, as Grandma put it. Then he went into Mom and Dad's bedroom with Dad, and Mom said nobody should disturb them since they were talking about something important.

"How come Uncle Jack's acting so crabby?" Jelly Bean asked Mom.

Just then Joel came downstairs. "You can't see he's upset about Suzanne?" he asked Jelly Bean in a mean voice.

"I know that," she said and narrowed her eyes at him.

"Then why did you have to ask?" he said, shaking his head.

Jelly Bean went to watch TV on the couch in the den with Britney. A really dumb movie was on, and everyone in it had weird accents and it was impossible to understand what they were saying. She and Britney huddled underneath the soft cuddly blanket on the couch. "Ew," she said to Britney after a couple of minutes, "this blanket smells."

"Don't forget your uncle was lying on it last night Jel," said Britney.

"Peuh!" said Jelly Bean, throwing it off. Roger-Over jumped up on the couch and licked them both, first one then the other. Jelly Bean and Britney laughed. He must have thought they were playing some kind of game with the blanket. When Uncle Jack and Dad finally came downstairs and went into the kitchen, Jelly Bean and Britney got up and followed them. Uncle Jack sat down at the table. Jelly Bean draped her arms around him from behind, and put her cheek next to his. "Ew, you smell," she told him, jumping back. Britney's arm was draped around Jelly Bean's shoulders.

"Guess I could stand to take a shower," said Uncle Jack, turning around to face her and Britney. He smiled, and looked a little more like his old self again.

"Eat something first," Mom told him.

"All right then, I guess I'll have that bagel and butter."

"What happened last night with you and Suzanne anyway, before you came over?" asked Jelly Bean, leaning over him.

Uncle Jack looked down at his plate. He pushed away the bagel Mom had put in front of him. He sat at the table with his arms folded. Everyone looked upset. Mom turned around from the sink and gave her an unhappy look.

"What?" said Jelly Bean, tears springing into her eyes. "What did I say that was so bad?"

"Idiot," Joel muttered under his breath. He was standing in the corner of the kitchen, either texting someone or playing one of his dumb games on his phone.

"Shut up!" said Jelly Bean, and went to hit him.

"Come here," said Britney, grabbing her arm and dragging Jelly Bean back into the den. Roger-Over padded after them, and sat in front of the girls next to the couch.

"What did I say that was so terrible?" Jelly Bean asked Britney. She put her head down on Britney's lap, covered her eyes and started to cry. "Everyone around here hates me," she sobbed. "For no reason!" she cried out.

"I think your uncle's probably not ready to talk about what happened yet," Britney told her in a soft voice. She was obviously the only one who cared about her.

"But why not? We always talk about things together," Jelly Bean said between sobs. She sat up and blew her nose.

"I know, but he's really hurt Jel. That makes it hard to talk." Britney went to get some more tissues from the bathroom, and handed them to Jelly Bean.

"I'm hurt too," she told Britney, sobbing away.

"I know," Britney told her, "but it's different. You should have seen my mom after she had a couple of break-ups with boyfriends that didn't work out. She was a basket case for weeks after."

"Is that how you know so much about all this?" asked Jelly Bean. She blew her nose so hard it sounded like the loud honk of a car, and that made them both crack up laughing again.

"Well," said Britney, "I guess it's all from things that happen all around me. Not just crazy things that go on with my mom. Jel, I know we live right near each other in the same town, but it's different in my neighborhood. I mean, the kids are the same as you and your brothers in a lot of ways, but where I live the kids kind of grow up faster." Jelly Bean was staring at her. "I need to go home soon," she told her.

"Okay," Jelly Bean said, looking down at the floor. Britney gave her a hug. "You'll be okay. Everything will all work out in the end, one way or another. My mom says that a lot, and she's always right."

"Don't go Brit," said Jelly Bean, even though she knew Britney had to leave.

"My mom wants to spend a little time with me. She texted me just before and asked when I was coming home."

"All right," said Jelly Bean, "if you really have to. I guess your mom deserves to spend some time with you." They both laughed. "You're the best, Brit," she told her. They went into the kitchen with their arms around each other, and Jelly Bean asked Dad if he could please take Britney home now. He said he would, in just a minute.

Mom was on her phone with Grandma. She told Grandma to hold on for a minute. "Jilly, Grandpa isn't feeling well again, so they can't come to take you skating. His doctor said he needs to rest, and Grandma doesn't want to leave him alone." It looked like Mom was going to be on the phone for a while. She talked to Grandma a lot now, because Grandpa hadn't been feeling good.

When she got back from taking Britney home with Dad, Jelly Bean went up to her room to talk things over with Roger-Over. "Roge, it's lonely when Britney leaves." She lay on her bed on her stomach, and reached down to stroke his back. "I used to be happy when Taylor left," she told him. Jelly Bean rolled over onto her back, and looked up at the ceiling. "I couldn't wait to be by myself again. And that time Heather came over, I *really* couldn't wait till she left."

Jelly Bean turned on her side to look down at Roger-Over. She stroked his tail, then picked some crusty stuff out of the corners of his eyes and examined his ears. They felt like velvet, but inside they were like little bony mazes. He whined and tried to get away, so she finally stopped and rolled back on her bed. "Britney is the first friend I've ever had who's really fun to be with. All the time." After staring at Roger-Over for a few minutes and feeling sorry for herself, Jelly Bean noticed the script of the play sticking out from underneath her desk. She jumped up to get it and that made Roger-Over scramble up and follow her to her desk. His bandaged leg looked like it was dragging a little bit after him.

"Roge," said Jelly Bean, plopping back down on her bed with the script, "do you know I even got a little jealous when Britney said she had to get home to spend some time with her mom? That's silly, right? Of course, she needs to be with her, she's her mom! But it sounds like they have so much fun together. That made me feel a little bad." Jelly Bean worked on braiding the strings that hung down from her bedspread.

"I mean, it's not that I don't have fun with Mom," Jelly Bean told him, "it's just that, well maybe we just haven't done anything that much fun together lately. And maybe they have more fun together because she doesn't have a dad. But why would I be jealous of someone who doesn't have a dad?" It didn't make sense. She thought about it while braiding the tassels at the end of her bedspread. She thought some more about it while she made a paper airplane out of the first page of the script. "But it kind of does make sense, Roge."

"Yikes," said Jelly Bean, trying to flatten out the page she had made into an airplane. "Okay, I feel better. You're a good listener," she told Roger-Over, leaning down to stroke his silky coat. He looked up at her, and Jelly Bean was sure he was smiling. "Now it's down to business." She sat up straight at her desk and repeated every one of Marlowe's lines over and over until she had memorized her whole part. Finally she didn't have to look at the script even once. Next, she checked to see who was online. Nobody she really felt like talking to. Or anyone who wanted to talk to her, either. So she put two new songs on her iPod and danced around to each of them.

"Come on Roge," Jelly Bean said. "Let's go outside. Maybe Dad'll take a walk with us." Dad had fallen asleep in his chair with the newspaper on his lap. It was turned to the crossword puzzle page. "Dad," said Jelly Bean, jumping on his lap. "Wake up! It's the middle of the day."

"Ooh!" said Dad, grabbing his stomach and catching his newspaper before it fell off his lap.

"Good catch," said Jelly Bean. "Come on, let's go for a walk."

Dad was fun to walk with. He joked a lot, and was happy to talk about whatever Jelly Bean wanted to talk about. Well, most of what she wanted to. "Is Grandpa going to be okay?" she asked him.

"I hope so, Jilly," said Dad. "I really do."

"Dad, I miss Britney when she leaves. I never felt that way about any other friend before. Or anybody who ever came over to play." Some of them weren't exactly friends, she thought to herself. She skipped around the living room while Dad looked for his other shoe.

"You're lucky when you find a good friend, Jilly. Good friends aren't always easy to come by."

"That's the problem I've been having," Jelly Bean told him. "Hey, do you want to hear my lines?" she asked him.

"You mean for the play?" Dad asked, when they got outside.

"They're really Marlowe's lines," said Jelly Bean. "But I've been learning them just in case she doesn't memorize them in time. Or in case she's sick the day of the play. She's been absent."

"Sure, I'd love to hear them," Dad answered. "But Jilly—"

"I know, I know," said Jelly Bean. "I might be learning them for nothing." She was sick of everyone telling her the same thing.

"As long as you know that," said Dad.

"I do," said Jelly Bean. She said all her lines, and Dad listened. Even though it looked like he had taken out his phone a few times to check his emails.

"Impressive Jilly," said Dad, when she was done.

"Thanks Dad," said Jelly Bean. They put their arms around each other, which was a little awkward with Dad holding onto his phone, and Jelly Bean holding Roger-Over's leash. He was trying to get free to chase after a squirrel. "Whoa!" she told him. After a little while Dad said he had to get back, because he needed to finish up some work for one or two of his clients. He also needed to call Mom to find out how Grandpa was doing.

When Jelly Bean got back Sam had just come in, so Jelly Bean followed him upstairs to his room. "I haven't seen you in ages," Jelly Bean told him, and plunked down on the other bed in his room. It was all squishy, so she couldn't resist bouncing up and down on it.

"I found out something," Sam said softly. He pulled over his desk chair, turned it around, and sat on it facing Jelly Bean. "I heard Mom talking to

Grandma about Uncle Jack. I kept looking down so it looked like I was texting and not like I was listening. She was talking in that soft voice that means you don't want anyone to hear you, but I think I figured it all out." Sam spun around in his chair. He grabbed his guitar from the floor. "But if I tell you, you have to swear you won't tell anyone."

"Okay I won't," said Jelly Bean, bouncing up and down on the bed. "You know I won't, Sam. And please don't start treating me like a baby, like everyone else around here does," she added.

"All right, I'm sorry," said Sam. "So Uncle Jack's friends, the ones who brought him here last night, called Grandma and Grandpa, and told them the reason he got so drunk last night was because of what Suzanne did to him."

"What did she do to him? Why did they have to call Grandma and Grandpa about it?"

"His friends must have thought they ought to know."

"Oh," said Jelly Bean. "He was acting pretty crazy last night, chasing around Pia and knocking everything over. It was weird. And scary," Jelly Bean told him. "I was glad Britney was here. She's seen drunk people acting crazy before."

"I guess that must have been the first time you ever saw anyone drunk and acting like a lunatic."

"Yeah, it was. But then he fell asleep on the couch," Jelly Bean told him.

"He passed out."

"So," Jelly Bean asked, taking a tennis ball off Sam's floor and throwing it up and catching it a few times, "why did Uncle Jack decide to get drunk and chase Pia all over the place? How did that help him?"

"The getting drunk part was because he took Suzanne to a party last night, and then she went home with another guy," Sam explained. "The chasing around Pia part I guess was because he was imagining she was Suzanne."

"How come she didn't just go to the party with the other guy in the first place?" asked Jelly Bean. Sam shrugged. "Wait," she said, "did Suzanne change her mind about getting married to Uncle Jack?" she asked. She began to realize what that awful Suzanne had done, and started to understand more about what had happened to Uncle Jack.

"Guess she didn't really love him after all," Sam explained.

"Then why did she tell him she would marry him?" Jelly Bean asked.

"Probably because she was just using Uncle Jack to get this other guy jealous."

"At least we don't have to see her anymore," said Jelly Bean. "I'm happy about that."

"Always good to look on the bright side," said Sam, grabbing his guitar and plunking down on his bed with it. He started strumming some chords that sounded like the beginning of a popular song.

"Can't he find somebody else to marry him?" Jelly Bean asked. "Not someone awful like Suzanne?"

"I'm sure he can," said Sam. "But he really thought she loved him. Now he might not trust other girls. Other women, that is."

"Oh," said Jelly Bean, "but he should pick out somebody better, who wouldn't just go home with someone else from a party. That's really mean."

"I know," said Sam. "But as they say, 'all is fair in love and war.'" He strummed the tune a little louder.

"Who says that?" asked Jelly Bean.

"It's an expression," said Sam. "And anyway, like you said, if she hadn't ditched him, we'd have to have her as our aunt."

"That's true," Jelly Bean agreed.

"He'll be okay," said Sam, going over to open his backpack.

"But why did Uncle Jack get tricked by her?" Jelly Bean asked. "I mean let himself get tricked."

"She's pretty good-looking, don't you think?" Sam asked.

"Yes," Jelly Bean answered slowly, not exactly sure what that had to do with the question she had asked.

"A guy can be tricked pretty easily," Sam told her, "if a girl's good-looking. Just like a girl can be tricked if a guy's good-looking."

"But why?"

"That's not so easy to explain," he told her. "It's just how it goes sometimes."

"Oh great," said Jelly Bean. "So that's the reason people get drunk?"

"It's one of the reasons," he told her.

"Oh," said Jelly Bean. "Thanks for explaining things to me, Sam." For a long time after she went back to her room, she kept thinking about how a mean girl who was nice-looking had tricked Uncle Jack.

Chapter 14

In Which Jelly Bean Becomes More Popular, She Memorizes All Marlowe's Lines in the Play, Marlowe's Absent, and they Can't Help Hoping She's Absent the Day of the Play. Taylor's Behavior Worsens. And Joel Is Annoying as Ever.

The next day, Taylor wasn't in school. At lunch, some of the girls were saying she had been suspended from school for a whole week. Others said she had only been suspended for a few days – some said two, and some said three. Everyone was arguing about it. No one really knew for sure.

Ms. Peiser told everyone that now they had to go full steam ahead with play rehearsals. Jelly Bean stood on the stage as a tree, and felt so dumb. Marlowe knew her lines perfectly, even better than any of the other main parts did.

Mom picked up Jelly Bean and Olivia after school.

"So," said Mom, after she dropped off Olivia, "did Taylor really take pictures of some of the girls in the bathroom?"

"She did, Mom."

Mom shook her head. "What happened to her, did she get suspended?" She looked over at Jelly Bean.

"Didn't her mom tell you why she wasn't going to be in school for a few days?" Jelly Bean answered.

"Not exactly," said Mom, slowly. She pursed her lips. "Sad what happened to that little girl. She was always allowed to get her way."

When they got home, Jelly Bean trudged upstairs from the garage with her backpack on her back. It was really heavy this year.

"How about a snack?" Mom asked.

"Okay," said Jelly Bean. Mom brought her some grapes and cut-up melon. "You think I'm getting fat?"

"No, I don't think you're getting fat," said Mom, giving her a funny look and shaking her head. She gave Jelly Bean a hug. "Just thought you might want something healthy. Besides, it's close to dinnertime."

Jelly Bean gave Mom a big hug. "I love you," she said, burying her head in Mom's stomach.

"Love you more," said Mom. She answered that way a lot. "And why would you ask me if I think you're getting fat?" Mom looked up from going through the mail.

Jelly Bean ate some of the fruit. "Just now some of the girls in school talk about getting fat, that's all," she told Mom.

Mom barely answered. Instead, she ripped open a piece of mail that looked like a bill and stared at it for a little while. "I'm sorry Jilly, what?" said Mom.

"Nothing," said Jelly Bean. She really wanted to talk to Mom about Uncle Jack, but just then the front door banged open and Joel and one of his loud friends burst in. "That's my cue to leave," she told Mom, who looked like she wasn't paying much attention to her anymore anyway. "Come on Roge," she called outside. "Let's go up." He was happy to follow her upstairs. Roger-Over was a pal. He always had time for her.

On Wednesday, Taylor was back in school. The whole time they walked to the classroom together after they were dropped off, Taylor talked loudly about what she had done while she was suspended from school.

"My mom took me to the mall, and I got a ton of clothes. And new shoes and boots. Then I got a new rug for my room. It's all white and fluffy. Then I picked out some new computer games, so I wouldn't be bored. I bugged my mom till she gave in—"

"Hi Jel!" Britney called out. She was with Shelby, Riley and Reese, and they all came over to crowd around Jelly Bean.

"Listen," Taylor called out, grabbing the sleeve of Jelly Bean's sweater. "I'm not done!"

"Stop," Jelly Bean said quietly to her, turning around, while the others surrounded her and were acting like they needed to tell her something. "Taylor, you're going to tear my sweater," Jelly Bean told her. She was trying hard not to be mean to Taylor, even though Taylor didn't make that easy. Jelly Bean still felt bad for her. She knew how it felt to not have any friends.

"Guess what?" everyone was saying to Jelly Bean at once, as she stood inside the doorway of the classroom. "Marlowe's absent!"

"Oh," said Jelly Bean. Then all of a sudden, she realized what that meant. "Oh!" she said a little louder, as they all hugged and jumped up and down together into a tight little knot. "But that doesn't mean she'll be absent next week," Jelly Bean said more seriously, looking around at all the girls' faces. Did they all really care whether or not she ended up getting Marlowe's part in the play?

So it seemed like when one popular girl acted a certain way toward someone, everyone else just fell into line behind her. Jelly Bean knew she'd never be getting so much attention from the other girls if Britney hadn't started paying attention to her. Everyone was taking off their jackets and quickly putting their backpacks and lunches away. Ms. Peiser called out that they had two more minutes to get to their seats.

"We hope she stays absent," said Britney, in a serious voice, putting her arm around Jelly Bean, and resting her head on Jelly Bean's shoulder.

"So do I," said Sophie. "You'd be much better than her in that part."

"But I don't want her to be really sick or anything," said Jelly Bean, suddenly feeling worried. She didn't want to hope for someone to be out sick. But still, she decided she could wish for her to have to go away with her family on an unexpected trip, or something like that.

"We heard you know all her lines," said Greer.

"And we also found out why you were late, the day Ms. Peiser gave out all the parts," said Shelby sympathetically. "That was unfair. I think we should all talk to her." *How embarrassing,* thought Jelly Bean, feeling herself turn red. Now everyone must know that she had fallen in the toilet that day, probably even the boys.

"Listen, I don't hope Marlowe's sick or anything like that—" Jelly Bean tried to tell them all. But now the classroom had gotten so noisy, with everyone rushing to their seats, scrambling around trying to do their daily jobs, this one giving out lunch tickets, that one scribbling something on the board, someone else fixing the calendar, that no one looked like they were listening to her anymore. Everyone was struggling to get homework out of backpacks. And since most of the boys' backpacks were a big mess of scrunched up papers and books, this always led to papers pouring out all over their desks and onto the floor. Jelly Bean wondered how they ever found anything they were looking for. A few of the girls' backpacks were just as bad, she noticed.

"Are you coming to my house this weekend, Jelly Bean?" Taylor called out from across the room. She was trying hard to get from her seat to Jelly Bean's, but everyone she tried to pass was blocking her path. They were either getting out their books, or leaning over, or talking to someone else, or just plain in the way for one reason or other. "Can you move!" Taylor yelled at Dylan, who was one of the slowest boys in the class to get organized. In fact, he managed to be the last one to get his desk set up every day. Ms. Peiser often asked one of the girls to help him because his situation always looked so hopeless, and he often looked like he was about to cry. He was always pulling a mess of crumpled papers out of his backpack. Still, it must have been embarrassing to have to have one of the girls help him every day.

"Miss Alpert, come up here, please." Ms. Peiser sounded angry, and was shaking her head. Taylor sighed a loud sigh, and everyone stopped what they were doing to look at Ms. Peiser. She lowered her head, and covered her eyes with her hand. "All right, that's it," she finally said. "Does anything have an effect on you?" she asked. In total silence, everyone waited for Taylor to get to the front of the room. "Bring all your things up here. This is where you're going to sit for the rest of the day." Ms. Peiser motioned to the small area behind her desk.

The whole class whispered and buzzed. "The next move," Ms. Peiser scolded Taylor, "will be putting your desk out in the hall. And your parents will be called. Again." She sat down at her desk and began to take attendance. "No need to take up any more valuable class time dealing with one person's bad behavior."

Everyone sat down. All you could hear were chairs shuffling into place. Then even that stopped. Someone dropped a pencil. Other than that, the room was quiet.

Right after the pledge, Ms. Peiser told the class that at play rehearsal she was going to assign someone to stand on the stage where Marlowe was supposed to stand, and read her lines from the script.

"Jillian knows all Marlowe's lines by heart," Reese piped up. A lot of the other girls clapped and cheered.

"Boo!" said a lot of the boys, but some of the girls said a few not nice things to them and they stopped.

Ms. Peiser chewed on her lower lip for a little and then said that all right, she'd let her say Marlowe's lines. The whole class walked to the auditorium.

Jelly Bean's heart was thumping the whole way. She and Britney held hands tightly. A lot of the girls were smiling at her while they walked, and some of them skipped alongside the two of them. Taylor tried to push past everyone to walk closest to Jelly Bean, but Jelly Bean was too busy saying the lines to herself to even notice that other people were pushing Taylor away.

"Some best friend!" Taylor finally called out loudly.

"You call YOURself a best friend?" Britney asked Taylor. "Joke, right?" She squeezed Jelly Bean's hand. Jelly Bean smiled at her. "Nervous?" Britney asked. Jelly Bean nodded. "You shouldn't be," Britney told her.

Ms. Peiser told Taylor to come to the front of the line. Taylor groaned. Jelly Bean felt bad for Ms. Peiser. Sam had told her there was always one kid in every class who made the teacher's life miserable. It never failed.

After rehearsal – at lunchtime – Ms. Peiser took Jelly Bean aside. "Jillian, I have no idea whether or not Marlowe will be back in school by the day of the play. You know it's only a week away. I don't know why she's absent today, but I know she is excited about her part. I'm telling you this so that you don't let yourself become terribly disappointed."

"I'll really try not to," said Jelly Bean.

"You did do an excellent job memorizing all her lines," said Ms. Peiser.

"Memorizing isn't that hard for me," Jelly Bean told her.

"I see," said Ms. Peiser.

Mr. Singer came over to where Ms. Peiser and Jelly Bean were talking. He stood next to them, holding his tray. He looked way down at Jelly Bean, the same way Ms. Peiser was looking down at her, but from much higher up. Mr. Singer had a nice smile, Jelly Bean noticed, and his teeth were shiny white. He was really skinny. Joel had had him as a teacher when he was in fifth grade, and said he was a great teacher. But what did Joel know? He probably liked him because he knew a lot about sports, and liked talking to the kids about basketball, football and baseball teams, and all that kind of thing.

"I'll try not to get my hopes up too much Ms. Peiser," said Jelly Bean. *But I'm not sure I can do that*, she said to herself.

"All right, Jillian," Ms. Peiser told her. "Go finish your lunch." She gave Jelly Bean a big smile. Jelly Bean couldn't help noticing how different Ms. Peiser acted around Mr. Singer. She sounded much kinder and friendlier than usual.

In the afternoon, everyone had to form groups of either two, three, or four people tops, to work on a hobby. Devon was asked to be in a group with Riley and Reese, and Britney and Sophie came over to sit in the two desks next to Jelly Bean. Shelby turned her desk around and walked it over to join them. She made it look funny, and everyone laughed to see her desk moving towards the other girls.

"Please can I be the fifth person in that group, Ms. Peiser?" Taylor called out. Jelly Bean saw Taylor move from side to side, her head stretched forward, waddling up to Ms. Peiser's desk. "Just this one time?"

"No Taylor," Ms. Peiser answered, "I'm sorry, you cannot. No groups of five, they really don't work out." Taylor sat down with a thud. Her face was all red and she wore an angry expression. She folded her arms and her bangs flopped in her face.

"There are several groups with either two or three people in them," Ms. Peiser went on. "There is no need for you to make a fuss about this, Taylor. You see everyone else finding a group with the right number of people in it."

Taylor made an angry noise, something like a roar. Then she kept saying she didn't know what the big deal was. Ms. Peiser looked down and scribbled something on a piece of paper. "I need you to take this note home with you tonight, and bring it back to me tomorrow signed by one of your parents," she told her. By now everyone in the class was buzzing. Bad behavior always got people's attention. Jelly Bean noticed that Heather was in the group Taylor finally joined. Then she watched as Taylor crumpled up the note Ms. Peiser had given her to take home, and threw it on the floor. Then Taylor put her head down on her arms on her desk, and every so often she stamped one of her feet on the floor.

Hobby hour was usually the most fun time of the week, but now Jelly Bean was having trouble concentrating. Everyone was supposed to turn to the "Hobbies" section of their notebooks, and plan a project to work on as a group. Their projects had to be related to one of their school subjects, and they had to decide how to share their results with the class. First though, Ms. Peiser had to approve each group's ideas. This was all supposed to teach everyone to be creative and also how to work together as a team.

Sophie and Britney were talking about writing down the names of as many animals as possible, and then listing them alphabetically. They were going to cut out pictures of animals from the magazines in the classroom, then draw the animals they couldn't find, and put together a children's dictionary all about animals.

Another group was going to make questionnaires to hand out to other students in the school, to find out how many students watched different TV shows. They were going to ask everyone how many hours they spent online, how many hours they usually spent on homework, add that information to the TV answers, and put the results on big pie charts.

A group of boys was drawing pictures of different places in New Jersey, and making a guidebook all about places they would recommend to kids to go to have fun and learn about new places. All the projects sounded clever to Jelly Bean. But when she tried to concentrate on her group's project, she just couldn't. She gave up trying to get her mind off the play. She tried to stop wishing for Marlowe to stay absent, but she couldn't help it.

The next day when Jelly Bean was eating breakfast, Joel made a nasty face at her before he headed out the door.

"He always tries to make me feel bad, Mom," Jelly Bean said. "I hate being the youngest. It's awful."

"I know it's difficult for you sometimes," said Mom, only this time she wasn't even checking her phone, which she said had been giving her problems. "It's not always easy for Joel either," she told Jelly Bean, giving her a hug and stroking her hair.

Jelly Bean hugged back, getting some cream cheese from her fingers on Mom. "I don't see what's so hard for him," she said. "He should be glad he's not the youngest in the family."

"That's from your point of view," said Mom. "He sees things from his side. He thinks you always get more attention than he does, being the only girl and all."

Jelly Bean took a last bite of her banana. "But he's never nice to me Mom, ever. And it's not true that I get more attention."

"You know what I hope, Jillian?" Mom asked. "I hope one day you both make up your minds to love each other and act nice towards each other. That's what would make me happy. And it would be rewarding for you both."

"Well then he can start being nice first," said Jelly Bean. She wanted to make Mom happy, but this was a lot to expect. Once again, this was not something adults could casily understand. Especially Mom. She couldn't possibly.

Olivia's Mom honked. Jelly Bean grabbed her backpack and lunch and gave Mom a hug before she ran out the door. She didn't know if she would ever be able to get along with Joel. He'd have to change a lot.

Chapter 15

In Which Jelly Bean Tries to Figure Out Cameron, Grandma and Grandpa Come for Dinner, and All Her Brothers Are so Different

Jelly Bean got home from school, grabbed a snack and went to walk Roger-Over right away. He was walking around in circles like he was desperate to go out. In the morning Mom had said she was going to have a long day in the city. On the way back from walking Roger-Over, Jelly Bean saw Grandma and Grandpa's car pull into the driveway. She started running up the street, but Roger-Over barked to remind her to slow down. "Sorry, old guy," she told him, "but I haven't seen Grandma and Grandpa in ages!" That's what it felt like, even though Jelly Bean remembered it had only really been a few days.

"Hi Grandma! Hi Grandpa!" Jelly Bean called, taking slower steps, but wishing she could run with Roger-Over like he used to be able to. She finally caught up to them, and Grandma and Grandpa each gave her a huge hug and lots of kisses.

"How's my Jillian?" Grandma asked in her most excited voice that sounded like a tinkling bell.

"We brought all your favorite things," said Grandpa, unloading grocery bags from the trunk of their car. "We brought you a turkey sandwich on rye, some M&M's, and some of those magazines you like."

"Yippee!" said Jelly Bean, taking one of the bags of goodies from Grandpa. "Mmmmmm," said Jelly Bean. The sandwich smelled so good. Grandma told him he shouldn't be carrying so much at one time.

"How do you feel, Grandpa?" Jelly Bean asked. "I hope you're all better." She grabbed his arm and jumped up and down a few times.

"Like a million bucks Missy," Grandpa answered. "Ready to play some cards?"

"Sure!" Jelly Bean answered. She went over to Grandma and they put their arms around each other. Still hanging on to Roger-Over's leash, she snuggled up against Grandma as they walked. Grandma always felt like one big mushy pillow. Grandpa went ahead of them, like always, balancing a gazillion things on each of his arms. Mom said Grandpa was born in a rush. She said he tried to do too many things, all at the same time, and he just didn't know how to slow down. Mom said all his rushing around was giving him problems with his heart. When Grandpa was ready to go back home, he would go out to the car while Grandma was still saying good-bye to everyone, and honked the horn till she came out. It was annoying, but Mom said he couldn't help it. She said Grandma gave up long ago trying to get him to change.

Michael, Cameron and Brady were on their way out the door. Cameron raced out the door so fast, she nearly tripped over Roger-Over.

"You don't say hello to your grandmother anymore, Michael Jason?" Grandma asked him. He stood still just long enough for her to stand on her tiptoes and give his cheek a big kiss. Then he surprised Grandma by grabbing her around her large waist and lifting her off the floor. Her eyes got as wide as Jelly Bean had ever seen them. "Whoa!" she called out. He put her down pretty fast.

"Where are you boys going?" Grandpa asked, "out for a spin?" Michael and Brady laughed. Grandpa loved joking around with the boys. He said it made him feel young again.

"Over Cameron's, Mr. Miller," Brady answered. "We have a school project we need to work on. She has all the supplies." They looked from one to the other, and smiled in a funny way. Jelly Bean looked from Grandpa to Michael to Brady, trying to figure out what secret they were all keeping from her.

"School project, huh? I know about those," said Grandpa, giving Brady a pretend punch in the arm. Grandpa laughed, and his whole face crinkled. Sometimes he laughed so hard he had to take out his handkerchief and wipe away tears from his eyes. This was one of those times.

"I'll be right back," Jelly Bean said to Grandma, running the few steps down to Brady's car, where Cameron was waiting in the passenger seat for Michael and Brady. She was scrunched down in the seat, twirling her hair, looking out the car window. Jelly Bean was a little afraid of Cameron, but still she bravely went around to the other side of the car and asked her through the half-open window, "Are you my brother's girlfriend?"

"No," she answered, blowing a gigantic bubble with her gum.

"Why?" she asked, popping her gum loudly.

Jelly Bean stared at her, confused. "Because you're always with him." Cameron looked straight ahead out the windshield, and sunk lower in her seat. Her hair was long and jagged. It hung down all over the front of her vest. Her arms and her neck had some strange-looking tattoos on them.

"Then are you Brady's girlfriend?" Jelly Bean asked. It just popped out. Like the other question had.

"Nope," Cameron answered, putting one foot up on the dashboard. She kept looking straight ahead. "We're friends, that's all. It works out better that way. No one gets hurt. The three of us just have a good time together, that's all."

"Oh," said Jelly Bean. She tilted her head and kept staring at Cameron, especially at the black and red tattoo on her ankle. Then she saw the smashed-up pack of cigarettes next to Cameron on the seat. "You shouldn't smoke," she said finally.

"No kidding," said Cameron. "I keep trying to quit, but I can't. Guess I don't want to badly enough, huh?"

"It's really bad for you," said Jelly Bean. "Do you watch the commercials on TV about it? They're on all the time."

Cameron shrugged her shoulders. "Yeah I know, you can't miss them. They're pretty gross." She looked down. Jelly Bean wanted to walk away and get back to Grandma, but she felt glued to the spot. She just stood there watching Cameron light up a cigarette, smoke it, and then check her nails.

When Michael and Brady got to the car, Brady lifted Jelly Bean up – high up, over his head. Then he spun around, with her head bouncing against his back. "Hey," she called, "put me down!"

"Say please!" said Brady.

"Please put me down!" Jelly Bean cried. He finally did. She was so dizzy she almost fell. "I wasn't expecting that!" she said, and they all laughed.

Grandma and Grandpa were calling her from inside the front door.

"Coming!" Jelly Bean called back, as she walked to the house. The whole world felt like it was spinning around. "Be right there," she told Grandma and Grandpa, once she was inside. She ran upstairs to see what Sam was up to. Unfortunately, Joel was in Sam's room. He was showing him a bunch of baseball cards he had put in an album. Sam looked interested.

"Joel, Grandma and Grandpa are here you know," Jelly Bean said, standing in the doorway.

"So?" He didn't even look up. He wasn't giving up Sam's attention so quickly.

"Grandpa just told me he brought over a lot of new baseball cards for you," Jelly Bean told him.

"He did?" Joel asked. He ran out of the room so fast his album and a lot of loose cards fell on the floor, but he didn't even act like he cared. "I'll get those later," he called back to Sam.

"That wasn't nice," Sam told her, after Jelly Bean closed the door. He reached for his guitar and played a few chords. The ones he usually started out with. All of a sudden it felt like things were changing between them. "You know I always like to talk to you, Jilly, but if Joel's in the room, you should talk to both of us."

"I can't Sam," Jelly Bean told him. "You know how much Joel hates me. He thinks I'm a pain. He thinks I'm in the way."

"He doesn't hate you, Jel."

"Does so," Jelly Bean pouted. "And anyway, I hate him too."

"You could do something about that," Sam told her.

"He should try to change. It's harder for me. I'm the youngest."

"I'm trying to help you, Jell. He's your brother too, you know."

"Whatever," said Jelly Bean, going to the end of Sam's bed and tickling the bottom of his feet.

"Hey!" he said, kicking his foot, "Stop! And you know that's not a good answer."

"Cameron told me she's not Michael's girlfriend," said Jelly Bean. She needed to change the subject.

"I could have told you that." Sam strummed the strings of his guitar.

"She's not Brady's girlfriend either."

"I know," said Sam. "It's a little weird, I agree. I don't know what the three of them are up to. But who cares, really." He kept playing the chords he always played.

"But they're always together," said Jelly Bean.

"I think those three really do love each other," said Sam. "In their own way."

"Mom thinks Cameron has bad manners," Jelly Bean said.

"Well, she's different," said Sam. "Cameron marches to her own beat." He played some sour-sounding chords.

Jelly Bean stuck her fingers in her ears.

"Maybe her family's different from ours," Sam went on. "Maybe they don't care about manners so much." Jelly Bean thought over that possibility.

"Would you kiss a girl who wasn't your girlfriend?" Jelly Bean asked. "I don't mean like Mom or Grandma, but just a girl?"

"Just a girl?" Sam laughed.

"Don't laugh at me, Sam." Jelly Bean folded her arms. She felt her cheeks turning red.

"Anyway, I think Cameron's the kind of girl who just likes being with boys more than she likes being with other girls."

"Oh," said Jelly Bean. "I wonder why."

"Think about it," said Sam, putting his guitar aside and punching his pillow to make it comfortable to lie back on.

"I don't know," said Jelly Bean, staring at Sam. She thought as hard as she could, but couldn't think of a reason.

"A lot of people think guys are easier to deal with. Girls can be cruel."

"Do you have a girlfriend, Sam?" she asked after a few seconds.

Sam hesitated. "I don't know," he said finally, picking up his guitar again. "Sort of. Don't ask me that, Jel. Not right now, anyway."

Jelly Bean was puzzled. She wanted to ask more questions, but Sam didn't look interested in talking about this topic anymore. And now Grandma was calling them for dinner.

"Sam!" said Grandma, when they got downstairs. She reached up and gave his forehead a big kiss. "You don't have time to say hello to your grandmother anymore?" She grabbed both his cheeks, and when she finally let him go, they were all red.

Sam gave her a great big hug. "Sorry Grandma," he said. "I got involved talking to Jilly."

"All right Mister. I guess my big brothers were the same way with me. Well, much of the time." Grandma bustled around helping Mom with dinner, adding more meat or more vegetables to one pot or another, opening the oven to check on something that smelled delicious – which turned out to be her yummy apple pie. Then she wiped her hands on her apron. Grandma did so many things at once, she was like six people rolled into one. She looked a lot like Mom, only shorter and plumper, and with mostly gray hair. Mom said Grandma's hands were always busy. "We have such a delicious dinner all ready for you," Grandma told them. She always sounded just like Jelly Bean's old kindergarten teacher, who everyone agreed was the nicest teacher in the whole school.

After dinner Grandma helped Mom clean up. Then she and Grandpa gave everyone a big hug and said they had to leave. As usual, Grandpa went outside and waited in the car for Grandma. There he didn't stop honking the horn until she came out. And Grandma never did seem ready to say good-bye to Mom.

Jelly Bean went up to her room followed by Roger-Over, to finish her homework. She lay on her bed petting Roge just thinking about a few things before she got started on her homework, when Sam knocked and asked if he could come in.

"What's the matter with you now?" Jelly Bean asked him. Sam didn't look like his usual self. "What happened?"

Sam had his guitar with him, and he started playing the same chords he was always playing. Only this time they turned into a song Jelly Bean recognized. "I got a bad grade on my math test today," he finally looked up from his guitar and told her.

"That's why you're upset?" Jelly Bean asked him, sitting up. When Sam got upset – which wasn't often – Jelly Bean couldn't help getting upset right along with him.

"If I keep getting Cs on my math tests, I'll never get into medical school."

"But you're only in tenth grade," Jelly Bean said, trying to cheer him up, even though it looked like that wasn't going to work. "Mom said you have time to bring up your grades. I heard her tell you that."

"Yeah, but I haven't been doing that. I hate Mr. Campion," said Sam, emphasizing the word "hate." "Oh, never mind that, it's not his fault. I should go in for extra help." Sam sat down on the other bed in Jelly Bean's room, threw his guitar aside, and put his head in his hands. "It's my own fault. I have trouble with trig."

"Don't worry," said Jelly Bean, sitting down next to Sam and leaning her head on his shoulder. "You're going to start doing better. If you just make up your mind. At least that's what you always say to me."

"Thanks," said Sam, standing up. "You're a pal, Jilly."

Jelly Bean smiled and felt happier than she ever remembered feeling. "I know you can do it," she told him. "I believe in you!"

"Okay, okay, let's not get carried away." Sam got up. But he was smiling.

"How come Michael never worries about his grades?" asked Jelly Bean.

"Who knows?" said Sam. "Maybe he's better off being that way. Or maybe he just handles his emotions differently." Then Sam said if he wanted to start doing better in school, he'd better go finish up his homework, and he went back to his room.

For a little while Jelly Bean lay on her back petting Roger-Over and thinking about how her brothers were all so different. And how she was always going to love Sam the most.

Chapter 16

In Which There Is a New Girl in Class Named Kylie; How Because of Her Friendship with Britney, Jelly Bean Is Liked by the Popular Girls; and Taylor Continues to Misbehave

A new girl was in class on Friday. She was little, had long reddish-brown hair and a lot of freckles, and she barely spoke. When she did, she spoke softly, but she giggled with her mouth wide open, and she had the kind of giggle that made you want to laugh along with her. Her name was Kylie, and she had just moved to New Jersey from Pennsylvania. She told everyone that the ride here from their old house had taken seven and a half hours, and that this was the fourth time her family had moved since she was a baby. They had to move all those times because of her dad's job.

"I'll share with Kylie, Ms. Peiser," Taylor called out, when Ms. Peiser asked for a volunteer to share all her books with Kylie until she got her own.

"All right, thank you Taylor," said Ms. Peiser. She didn't look happy about it, but she must have been trying to be fair. Taylor had been the first one to raise her hand. Some of the girls looked at each other and rolled their eyes. Taylor looked around at everyone as if to say, "See? I can get attention for a good reason."

At lunch, when Jelly Bean walked by Heather Farrell's table, she saw Taylor sitting there with Kylie. Taylor was telling her in a loud voice not to eat the school lunch, because there were rats in the kitchen. Taylor was turning into a big liar. Kylie was looking around, as if she was hoping for someone to come rescue her. Her lunch was just sitting there, and it looked so good: tuna fish with potato chips and pickles, and a packet of vanilla, chocolate and strawberry ice-cream for dessert, that was just melting away.

Jelly Bean smiled at Kylie when she passed by on the way to the seat Britney had saved for her. When she sat down, she started to tell Britney how upset Sam had gotten about his bad grade, and how it was so weird that Michael didn't seem to care about his grades at all.

"I'm really different from my sister," said Britney, in every single way you could think of." She bit into her sandwich, then chewed for a little, and looked like she was thinking over this situation. "So I know what you mean," she told her. "But with my sister and me it could be because we had different dads."

"Oh," said Jelly Bean, not exactly sure how to respond to that, even though now she was getting used to some parts of Britney's life that were not the same as hers.

"I feel bad for the new girl," Jelly Bean said to Britney. They both looked over at Kylie. She was swinging her legs back and forth under the table and not eating. Taylor looked like she was just about shouting in her face.

"Bet she wishes she could be anyplace else," said Britney. They looked at each other, and then they both turned around to face Kylie and smile at her. Taylor kept talking loudly right in Kylie's face, and Kylie looked as miserable as anyone could look. "We should try and rescue her," said Britney. Jelly Bean felt like she and Britney were often thinking the same thing at the same time.

"It must be awful to be new," said Jelly Bean. She lay her wrist on the table, and Britney put her wrist next to hers. They had matching friendship bracelets on, made with thin red string and tiny wooden beads that were lots of different bright colors.

"I like those," said Shelby, looking at their bracelets from across the table. Just as on most days, she was surrounded by Reese and the other girls who were always trying hard to keep being her friend. They always dragged their chairs over to be near Shelby during lunch, knowing the teacher on cafeteria duty was only going to tell them they had to move their chairs back. And day after day they looked so unhappy when they were told they had to go back to their original seats.

"Thanks, Shel," Britney answered, looking down at their bracelets and then at Jelly Bean. "We just got them." Shelby smiled. It was funny, but Jelly Bean couldn't help thinking of all the times Shelby had never paid any attention to her at all, but that was before she became best friends with Britney. It felt good to be noticed by Shelby, although Jelly Bean couldn't explain to herself exactly why that was.

When Taylor got up to throw out her lunch, she made a detour on the way back to her table and stopped right near Jelly Bean and Britney. "Hi Jel," she called out loudly.

"Oh hi, Taylor," Jelly Bean answered, trying to sound as nice as she possibly could. Over her leggings Taylor was wearing a top with lots of little silver circles on it that looked like coins. She was wearing bracelets with the same kinds of coin-things on them, and earrings that matched. Her whole outfit was making a lot of noise whenever she moved.

"Are you supposed to be dressed like a gypsy or something?" Britney asked her. "Maybe you didn't get the memo that Halloween's over."

Taylor laughed loudly. "My mom said I look like a model," she answered.

"Oh, okay," said Britney, giving Taylor a disgusted look and shaking her head. "Do you think it's nice to leave Kylie all alone at your table?" she asked her. "She's brand-new here, you know."

"She knows I'm coming right back," Taylor said. She twirled back to her seat, like she was trying to look like a model on a runway. "I'm coming Kylie, don't worry," she cupped her hands around her mouth and called out. Some boys and girls laughed, but others, like Shelby, shook their heads and looked disgusted. Shelby whispered something to Riley, but it was a loud whisper. Jelly Bean couldn't make out exactly what she said, but she was pretty sure it was something not very nice about Taylor.

"How about coming to my house tomorrow, Jelly Bean?" Taylor called out right when the bell rang, in a voice loud enough for everyone to hear. Luckily, though, in another minute the hall was jammed with everyone either racing, dilly-dallying or just plain walking back to class. Taylor pushed her way over to Jelly Bean, and tried to sound like they were still good friends. Jelly Bean wanted to stay away from her, but at the same time she did feel a little sorry for Taylor.

"I don't think so, Taylor," said Jelly Bean, "maybe another time." Taylor gave Jelly Bean a mean look, but Britney put her arm around her, and together they sped ahead and sailed past every boy and girl in the hallway, zig-zagging in between the ones who were going fast and the ones who were going slow. And they were the first ones to make it back to the classroom.

When they got inside, they leaned against the wall, wiped the sweat off their foreheads, and panted until they could catch their breath. Then they turned to face each other and started giggling like two crazy people.

After another minute or two everyone else piled into the classroom, including Taylor, who was dragging poor Kylie by her sleeve. "If you come over, we could play all my computer games," Taylor called out to Jelly Bean, while everyone was scurrying back to their seats. "My mom could take us to the mall – or to the movies – anything you want, Jelly Belly."

A few girls were crowded around Shelby's desk, looking at pictures of her new dog on her phone. They were saying "aw" and "he's so cute" and things like that. In another corner of the room Brandon was crying, because someone had pushed him into Cooper, and they had bumped heads really hard. Ms. Peiser was standing with Brandon asking him some questions, like did he feel dizzy or nauseous. Finally, she decided they both needed to go to the nurse, so she quick wrote out notes for them. Ms. Peiser raced back to her desk, even running a little in her too-high tan heels, and yelled "Everyone sit down now!" to the crowd around Shelby's desk. Everyone scattered to their desks. Shelby put her phone back in her pocketbook.

"Stop!" Jelly Bean mouthed to Taylor, who had come over to her desk to keep trying to talk her into coming over on Saturday. "You're going to get me in trouble," she added. Jelly Bean turned around in her chair to face the front.

"You're mean, you know that?" Taylor called out to Jelly Bean, and stomped to the back of the room. By then everyone was totally quiet, facing front. Taylor plunked down so hard in her chair that two of her books fell on the floor. So did her pocketbook, and everything in it went flying and rolling all over the floor.

Ms. Peiser just shook her head, and told Taylor to pick up her things and hurry up about it. She told her the next time she did anything to distract the class, she was going to get another detention, no two ways about it. Ms. Peiser rested the back of her hand on her forehead, and then straightened herself up.

Jelly Bean turned around and watched Taylor pick up all the junk from her pocketbook, fold her arms on her desk, and put her head down. Jelly Bean wondered why she had about 12 lipsticks in there, since she never wore any of them.

Ms. Peiser told the class to open up their social studies books, and announced they were going to go over what would be on the test about the Revolution. But it was difficult to concentrate. It was too tempting to keep turning around to watch Taylor who was sitting with her head down on her desk, her hair spread all over the place in front of her. A few other people kept looking around too, and they also tried not to make it obvious. It looked like Taylor was crying. Her shoulders and the top of her head were shaking and she stamped her feet a few times.

Jelly Bean looked out the window and rested her chin on her hand. She thought about all the good times she and Taylor had had together when they were little, how they used to run through the sprinkler in the summer, make giant piles of leaves in the fall to jump in, and huge snow tunnels in the winter – with Dad's help – to crawl through together. Michael, Sam and Joel used to join in too. Taylor did used to be a lot of fun. Everything was so different now...

Outside the window Jelly Bean watched a mom walking her baby in a stroller on the playground. The woman sat down and picked up her baby, who had started crying. Then she fed her baby inside her coat, and just like magic the baby calmed down. Once Jelly Bean had seen one of Mom's cousins do that upstairs in Mom and Dad's room when she was at their house, but everyone acted like it was a big secret. Mom had told everyone her cousin Ruth needed some privacy and not to go in.

"Jillian!" Ms. Peiser called out, causing Jelly Bean to almost jump out of her seat. It felt like she had gotten a shock, like when you touched a light switch by accident while you were moving on the carpet.

"I'm sorry, Ms. Peiser," Jelly Bean said, her heart beating a mile a minute. Tears sprang into her eyes, and her face felt hot all over. She leafed through her social studies book trying to find the right page. Britney tilted her book towards Jelly Bean to try to show her the page they were on, but Jelly Bean couldn't see quite that far.

"I don't know what has gotten into everyone today," said Ms. Peiser in her angriest voice. She emphasized the "what." "I do know that several people are going to have their parents called, and they will have to explain to me why it is becoming so difficult to behave appropriately."

Jelly Bean put her elbows on her desk and covered her eyes with her palms. She was trying hard not to cry, but now she couldn't stop. Mom would be so mad if she got a call from Ms. Peiser.

"Jillian, do you need a minute to go to the restroom to compose yourself?" Ms. Peiser asked.

Jelly Bean shook her head and straightened up. She was proud of herself for managing to pull herself together. Britney put one of her hands behind the other and gave her a hidden thumbs-up. She passed over a tissue, and Jelly Bean wiped her forehead and nose. She felt everyone's eyes on her, but she just stared down at a few words on the page her book was opened to.

Later, while everyone was waiting outside for their rides, Jelly Bean was standing with Britney and some of the other girls when she heard Taylor screaming at her across the yard. "Why don't you just say you hate me Jelly Bean? You know that's the reason you don't want to come over." She was dragging Kylie with her. When Taylor stopped right near Jelly Bean, Kylie pulled her arm free. "You got everyone else to hate me too," she yelled at Jelly Bean, even though now she was really close to her. Jelly Bean was too surprised to think of anything to say. So she just stared at Taylor with her mouth shut tight. Lots of girls and boys crowded around.

"You're a bully," Britney said to Taylor, grabbing Jelly Bean's hand. "If anyone does hate you, it's because you make them hate you. And stop blaming other people for things you do. Jelly Bean wouldn't make anyone hate anyone else. She's not that kind of person, and everyone knows it. Except you."

Jelly Bean was glad Britney stuck up for her, but she wished she had figured out something to say to Taylor on her own. She had known Taylor ever since they were babies. Now, though, the way she behaved was getting worse and worse. It was getting her in trouble all the time, and making everybody hate her. Britney was right that if anyone hated Taylor, it was her own fault. Mom had said that Taylor's parents should probably send her to a special school at this point. Taylor stood with her back to everyone, and waited for her mom. When she pulled up, Taylor stormed into the car, and Jelly Bean could imagine the way she must have been yelling at her mom. Jelly Bean was glad she had gymnastics that day.

The next day, Ms. Peiser had lunch duty. She called Jelly Bean over to her table, where she was sitting with Mr. Singer. "Jillian dear," she said in a honey-sweet voice Jelly Bean barely recognized. She leaned across Mr. Singer, who was sitting next to her and said to Jelly Bean, "I think it'd be a nice idea for you and some of the other girls to try to be Kylie's friend. It's not so easy, you know, for someone to make friends when she comes to a new school after the beginning of the school year."

It's not so easy to make friends even for a girl who does come in at the beginning of the school year, Jelly Bean felt like saying. She thought about what Sam had said about why Cameron liked being with boys better than girls.

Girls were tricky. You never knew exactly how they were going to behave next. Most of them, anyway. Then she noticed Mr. Singer looking at her with his head tilted to one side, sort of half-smiling.

"I'll try, Ms. Peiser," Jelly Bean said, "but—"

At that moment Britney came over and put her arm around Jelly Bean's shoulders. "Taylor's been hogging poor Kylie," Britney said, finishing Jelly Bean's sentence. "And it's really hard to make friends with someone who Taylor's hogging. If you know what I mean."

Mr. Singer burst out laughing. Ms. Peiser looked around at some of the other teachers, and they were all chuckling too. "We're not laughing at you girls," Ms. Peiser told them. "I'm sure you realize that."

"Oh yes she is!" one of the other teachers called out.

"Now ladies," said Mr. Singer. He and Ms. Peiser looked at each other as if they shared a secret of some kind. Jelly Bean wondered whether anyone else noticed the same thing.

"All right girls," Ms. Peiser said to Jelly Bean and Britney, "thanks. You can think about what we discussed. Now you can go back to your seats."

When they turned to walk away, Jelly Bean thought she overheard one of the teachers say something under her breath about Taylor that was not nice at all. "Oh lord," she heard Ms. Peiser say, and all the teachers giggled about whatever it was the teacher had said.

That afternoon they had play rehearsal. Marlowe knew her lines better than ever. Jelly Bean stood on stage the whole time, pushing the large cardboard boat back and forth that the scenery people had made. "A little less motion, Jillian," Ms. Peiser called out to her, in the middle of everything. Jelly Bean had been saying all Marlowe's lines to herself, so she didn't hear Ms. Peiser at first. "Jillian," she called out, putting her hands on both sides of her mouth, "wake up!" Some people laughed, but Ms. Peiser shushed them. Jelly Bean felt like an idiot.

Later on, while everyone was packing up to go home, Jelly Bean went up to Ms. Peiser to ask if Kylie could take her part in the play instead. But Ms. Peiser said no, because she felt Kylie was better off in the chorus, to be with a group of boys and girls. Jelly Bean said that if Kylie were on stage, she would get to know more people in the class. Ms. Peiser just gave her a look that said, "I know what you're up to, but forget it." Jelly Bean scrunched up her mouth, turned around and shuffled back to her seat.

After school, Sophie, Reese and Shelby walked outside with Jelly Bean and Britney. Kylie was walking just a short distance away from them, and Jelly Bean thought about saying something friendly to her like "See you Monday," or "I like your sneakers." But she was walking with all the most popular girls in the entire fourth grade, and it was too risky to say something they might think was dumb. Even though Britney did stick up for her a lot of times, still if Shelby or one of the others rolled her eyes at her, it would be too awful. She had too many recent memories of being so unpopular, and she didn't want to risk going back to that misery. She did smile at Kylie, but that was all. She tried not to think too hard about Kylie walking all by herself. Taylor wasn't with her, probably because she must have been back in the principal's office. For a change.

"I'm telling my parents not to come to the play," Jelly Bean said instead, because that's what was bursting to pop out.

"None of our parts are that great," said Shelby. Thank goodness, Jelly Bean thought to herself, Shelby decided to bother answering her. That meant she was part of Shelby's group. But Jelly Bean also knew that that could change at any time. It was even possible that Britney might decide not to be her friend some time or another. All these friends' situations were like tightropes in the circus where she had once gone with Dad, that the acrobats had to manage to stay on. She chuckled to herself, thinking that like the acrobats, all she had to do was stay balancing up there while she walked on that thin swaying rope.

"At least we each do have a few lines to say," said Sophie, who played Marlowe's daughter in the play. "Jelly Bean's right. Her part is really bad."

"You have more than just a few lines to say," said Britney to Sophie. "You have a really good part."

"It's such a dumb thing to fight about," said Shelby. No wonder she was the leader. The confident way she spoke made people want to be friends with her. "And after next Wednesday," she went on, "it won't matter at all."

"You should really try not to think about it," said Reese, patting Jelly Bean's shoulder. The funny thing was, Jelly Bean thought to herself, she did feel better. Now the most popular girls were trying to cheer her up, when just a few days ago she may as well have been invisible to all of them. Just a little distance away though, there was Kylie, standing all alone. That is, until Heather came along and Jelly Bean guessed that she was about to ask Kylie to come to her house that weekend. Heather was always on the lookout for new friends. She must have been hoping she could find someone else who still liked playing with dolls.

"Come on," Shelby called out, as everyone just stood around waiting, not doing much of anything. Jelly Bean whipped around at the sound of her voice. All the girls were waiting for Shelby to decide what everyone should be doing, thinking, and saying. Shelby put one arm around Riley and one arm around Reese, and everyone else in their group joined the three of them, putting their arms around the girls closest to them. Jelly Bean found herself right smack in the middle of Britney and Reese. She joined in as they all marched up and down the schoolyard, shouting: "One, two, three, four, five, six, seven, eight: WE ARE A LITTLE BIT CRAZY!" They kept doing it until some people saw their rides, yelled good-bye to everyone, grabbed their backpacks from the ground where they had thrown them, and ran to cars and buses.

This was the best day Jelly Bean had had in school so far this year, she decided.

Chapter 17

In Which Jelly Bean Is Asked to be in the States Gymnastics Competition, And Her Parents Tell Her She's Not Allowed to Go to Britney's House. Jelly Bean Is Not Happy About That, and Lets Them Know

That day after school Jelly Bean had gymnastics. Now Mrs. Clare almost always asked her to demonstrate each new move to the class. Today, in addition, she asked her if she could stay for a few minutes after class, and speak to her in her little private office. Jelly Bean asked Britney to wait for her in the lobby.

"Jillian," Mrs. Clare looked at Jelly Bean after everyone else had left, and said, "each year I have to choose one girl from this class to be in the States Competition. You may have guessed I'm going to ask you to be that girl, and I hope you'll think about it, discuss it with your parents, and say yes. Do you think you'd be interested?" Mrs. Clare sat very straight in her chair, her hand resting on the desk next to her. Her straight blond hair was pulled back in a tight ponytail, like always. Tiny beads of sweat sparkled on her forehead.

"I would like to," Jelly Bean answered. "Wow, thanks Mrs. Clare!" She wondered, for a minute, whether she was only imagining what Mrs. Clare had said. But it was real. There was Mrs. Clare, looking at her with a little smile, then glancing over at her laptop while she took a tissue and dabbed her forehead.

Mrs. Clare spoke with a foreign accent, and she pronounced everything carefully. "The first part of the exhibition isn't until March," she went on. I know that may sound like a long way off, but assuming your parents allow you to do this, we'll have to figure out time, between now and then, for me to help you learn a special routine, and for you to practice it. Do you think you would be able to schedule time for extra practices, Jillian?"

"Yes," said Jelly Bean, "yes I would, Mrs. Clare," she answered, although she did start wondering whether Mom might come up with reasons why she couldn't be in States. She might say it would take too much time away from her schoolwork. Or that it would be too much extra driving for her at dinner hour. You never knew with parents. You could never be sure which ideas they'd like, and which they wouldn't. Parents were funny that way.

"All right then," said Mrs. Clare, handing Jelly Bean the paperwork she had just printed out. She shut her eyes for a minute, and wiped her hand over her forehead. She covered her mouth and yawned a big yawn. "Let me know, Jillian, just as soon as you can, so I can pick someone else if you're not able to compete in this for any reason."

"Thanks, Mrs. Clare," said Jelly Bean, "I will." Then she scurried outside to find Britney and Mom.

"Wow," said Britney, after Jelly Bean told her the news. "Who cares if you have a stupid little part in the school play? Now you have something to really look forward to." She slung her arm around Jelly Bean. "I bet you end up in the Olympics!"

Jelly Bean opened her eyes wide and laughed. She and Britney hugged and jumped up and down together. No other girl would have cared that much about something good happening to her. And Britney was really and truly happy for her. Jelly Bean could tell.

"My sister – you know, Destiny," said Britney, "and her boyfriend are taking me to my mom's restaurant for dinner tonight. They're going to be here any minute."

"That sounds like fun Brit," said Jelly Bean. "You really think I could be in the Olympics one day?" She looked at Britney in a serious way.

"Girl, you gotta dream big," Britney told her. A car swerved and pulled up in front of them, honking loudly. "I have to go," she said. Destiny's boyfriend's car looked like an old heap of banged-up metal. "They're here." Britney ran to the car, her backpack flying behind her. She opened the door to the back seat and turned around to wave. She waved out the back window long after the car took off. Jelly Bean waved back. Britney got smaller and smaller. Such a little girl, Jelly Bean thought to herself, not even near grown-up size, and still she managed to help her in ways no adult could have.

"Jillian!" Mom was calling out her car window. "What are you doing? Didn't you see me here?"   Mom gave Jelly Bean a concerned look.

"Sorry, Mom," said Jelly Bean, when she got to the car, huffing and puffing. She threw her backpack into the back and hopped into the front. "Mrs. Clare asked me to be the one person in the class to compete in States," she announced, looking over at Mom.

"Wow Jilly," said Mom, sounding as if she was busy thinking about other things. "We'll have to discuss it."

"Why can't you just say okay?" All of a sudden Jelly Bean felt annoyed. Why couldn't Mom just be happy for her, the same way Britney was?

"I could try out for the Olympics after that, you know."

Mom turned to look at Jelly Bean. "I know how good you are in gymnastics, Jilly, and I know how much you love it. But I'm just not sure it's a good idea to commit to something that'll take a lot of time away from your schoolwork and other things you enjoy doing – like being in the play and relaxing on the weekends." She frowned. "And there's the danger too. When you start doing more complicated moves, you could fall and break something. Or something even worse than that."

"Oh boy Mom. So I guess you don't think I should dream big."

"I don't want you cracking your head open, Jillian," said Mom. "I prefer you in one piece."

"Other moms would be proud to have their daughters chosen to be in States."

"I am proud that you were asked, Jillian. But this mom is going to have to ask your dad, and we'll have to think it over."

"Then don't be surprised if I run away," said Jelly Bean. She looked out her window. It was dark and cold out now, but she could get some clothes packed up and leave first thing in the morning. She'd also need to wrap up some food.

"Would you come back to visit?"

"Maybe," said Jelly Bean, not sure whether to laugh or cry. "Maybe not."

"I'd miss you," said Mom, as they pulled into the driveway.

"Sure you would," said Jelly Bean, lugging her backpack and gymnastics bag out of the backseat. "You're just saying that to make me decide not to run away."

"That's funny," said Mom. "I used to say the same thing to my mom."

"So?" said Jelly Bean, scowling.

"Please don't be rude, Jillian," said Mom. "We've spoken about that. Anyway, Grandma used to offer to help me pack."

"Sorry Mom," Jelly Bean told her after thinking things over. "Grandma's funny. I know she really would have been upset if you had left."

When Jelly Bean got inside, Roger-Over ran downstairs – as fast as his leg let him – to lick her. He always made things better. She could never run away from home. It would be impossible to leave Roger-Over, and it'd be tough to take him along.

Later that night, when Mom came into her room to tuck her in, Jelly Bean asked if she could go to Britney's house on Sunday. "I mean in the afternoon, after Sunday school." Britney had texted her a little while ago to ask.

"Uncle Jack wanted to do something with you on Sunday, Jilly. He wanted to take you out to lunch and to that movie you wanted to see."

"No offense, Mom, but I'd rather hang out with Britney than Uncle Jack," Jelly Bean told her. "She's a lot more fun to be with than he is right now. And can you please check with me from now on, before making plans for me on the weekend? I'm not a baby anymore. I like to be the one to decide who I'm going to be with."

"All right, I will from now on," said Mom. "But I really thought you always enjoyed being with Uncle Jack." Mom took off her glasses and rubbed her eyes.

"I always used to, but I don't anymore Mom," said Jelly Bean. "He's not the same."

"He's been through a tough time," Mom told her. "Try to be understanding of him Jilly."

"I will try," said Jelly Bean, twisting under her covers from one side to the other. "I'll do something with him a different time. But this Sunday I really want to go to Britney's house. She's been here a few times, and now I want to go there. That's only fair," said Jelly Bean, leaning over to pet Roger-Over, who had just padded in. "We always have so much fun together, Mom. We're besties now."

"Jillian," said Mom, pursing her lips together and darting her eyes around the room, like she wasn't sure how to say what she wanted to say, "Dad and I would like it better if you weren't such good friends with Britney. At least we'd prefer it if you didn't go to her house," said Mom, looking down and staring at her nails. She looked up again. "But she's always welcome to come here."

Jelly Bean sat straight up. "Why would you say that Mom?" she asked, searching Mom's face and feeling her heart race like crazy. "Britney's my friend and I can go over to her house, just like she comes here," she said, putting her arms across her chest and holding them tight. Mom was going to have to change her mind. She just had to.

"I'm going to try to explain, Jill." Mom put her hand on Jelly Bean's shoulder, but Jelly Bean shrugged it away.

"Her mom's the type of person who has a lot of boyfriends," Mom explained.

"So what?" said Jelly Bean. "And it's because she doesn't want to be lonely," she yelled, hot tears clouding her eyes. "Britney explained all about that to me. And what does that even have to do with me and Britney? I don't care about her mom's boyfriends. And you shouldn't either!"

"Well," said Mom, clearing her throat, "I don't really think her home's a good environment for you to be in Jilly. I don't know how safe it is."

"Oh, like Taylor's home is such a great environment! Mom, she bosses around her parents like a little dictator. Her home is awful, and you always let me go over there. Her parents are afraid of her. You should see. She even curses at her parents – and they let her!"

"I know, honey, but some other kinds of things are more dangerous than others. It's hard to explain." Dad came in. He put his arm around Mom.

"Britney wasn't lucky enough to have a nice dad. Her parents had to get divorced. And now her mom wants to be with someone. She did have a lot of boyfriends, but the one she has now is really nice." Jelly Bean decided to leave out the part about Britney's dad being a hitter.

"Still, Jillian, it's someone her mom hasn't really known very long, and now he's around a lot. Most of the other mothers in the class feel the same way."

"I don't care what any of them think," Jelly Bean screamed. She grabbed a tissue and blew her nose. "Britney's my best friend, and that's all I care about. Not that you guys would understand. And she told me how the other mothers treat her mom. They're not nice to her at all. No one gives her a chance. Britney says they're all stuck up."

"How about if she comes here?" Dad suggested.

"No Dad!" Jelly Bean yelled. "How am I supposed to explain to her that I can't go there? She's already been over here a lot of times!"

"I'll help you figure that out," said Mom.

"You might have to end up telling her the truth," said Dad.

"Oh my god," Jelly Bean yelled, crying and then practically choking. "You're making me be the worst best friend in the whole world. Thanks a lot. You guys don't understand anything." She grabbed her pillow and shoved her head into it. She wanted to yell really loud. Joel pounded on the wall to tell her to be quiet. She had to scream back at him to shut up.

"Okay, so now I have to tell my best friend my parents think her house could be dangerous. After she was here the night Uncle Jack chased Pia all over the place like a drunken maniac." Jelly Bean grabbed her pillow and cried into it until it was soaked. Mom and Dad said a few more things that weren't helpful at all. They finally gave up and said good night. Life was so unfair. Mostly for kids.

What would she tell Britney? Jelly Bean thought about her running away idea, but realized quickly it probably wouldn't work out. She threw her sopping-wet pillow across the room and leaned over and petted Roger-Over for a while. Then she curled up in a ball and thought about why her favorite person in the whole grade had to have a mother who had boyfriends, and why did that even matter?

"It'll work out," said Dad, who came back in. Jelly Bean told him the rule about Britney was unfair, and he said he agreed with her about that, but that many things in life were unfair. Jelly Bean groaned. Dad stretched out on the other bed in her room, and he was snoring away in no time.

On Friday the plan was for Grandma and Grandpa to come pick Jelly Bean up in the late afternoon to take her to their house to stay overnight. At school that day, she had to make up a dumb excuse instead of telling Britney the truth about why she couldn't go to her house. Britney didn't seem surprised, and Jelly Bean had a feeling she knew the real reason. Jelly Bean felt sad for Britney, and she could tell this same thing had happened to her before, probably more times than Britney wanted to remember.

"Guess what?" Mom said later on, when she came into Jelly Bean's room to help her finish packing up her overnight bag.

"What?" she answered. Jelly Bean looked at Mom carefully, thinking maybe – just maybe – she had changed her mind about letting her go to Britney's on Sunday, after she got back from Grandma and Grandpa's.

"I got you the expensive jeans you wanted."

"I haven't talked about those in a long time," said Jelly Bean. Mom took the jeans out of the shopping bag she was holding and handed them to Jelly Bean. "Thanks Mom," said Jelly Bean. "You knew how much I wanted these." Everyone had them – Shelby, Reese, Riley, Sophie, Hadley, and of course Taylor – just about everyone who wanted to look cool and who could talk their mother into buying them. Britney didn't have them, but she had told Jelly Bean she didn't really care.

"We can call it an early birthday present," said Mom, "or an early Christmas present."

"It's okay," said Jelly Bean. "You can take them back. You don't have to waste your money. I don't really need them Mom, my old jeans are fine. And I don't really want them that badly. But thanks anyway." Mom looked at Jelly Bean in a funny way. She must have figured out that Britney was one of the few girls who wasn't going to get these jeans.

Mom folded the jeans carefully and put them back in the shopping bag. She sat down on the bed and put her arm around Jelly Bean. "I know you're disappointed Jillian about not being able to go to your friend's house. But I think you'll understand when you get a little older. Honestly, we moms try to make the best decisions for our kids." Mom looked down. "I don't know whether your friend told you that in her neighborhood a few teenage girls were jumped. Just last week."

Jelly Bean didn't say anything. She had overheard some people in the halls talking about that, but she had tried not to pay attention to what they were saying. Right now, she didn't want to think about it. And maybe those rumors weren't even true. She didn't want to have to look at Mom, so instead she kneeled down to tousle Roger-Over's fur. Then she put her head into Mom's stomach. "I still think you're not being fair," she told Mom, but it came out muffled. And even though she squeezed her eyes shut, tears filled them up and spilled over. Couldn't Mom understand that no matter what happened with Britney's mom or with girls who might have been jumped in her neighborhood, she still wanted to go to Britney's house? That was not going to change.

"I can't risk anything happening to you Jilly," said Mom. "That's what I need to worry about. I'm sorry you're unhappy." Mom sighed and got up to leave. Jelly Bean handed her the bag with the jeans, and Mom shook her head on the way out.

Jelly Bean lay there a long time, thinking. She'd have to think up a plan. She wasn't exactly sure what that plan would be, she just knew she had to think of one.